To Pemberley and Beyond

1813 EDITION

A Traveller's Guide to England by
the Bennets, Darcys, and Their Many Friends

By
Elizabeth Bennet Darcy,
Fitzwilliam Darcy, Esq.
with contributions by
the Bennets, Bingleys, Wickhams, Collins,
de Bourghs, and many others

Foreword by Jane Austen

Edited by Sarah Noelle James

THIS BOOK IS DEDICATED TO
THE INTREPID SOULS WHO YEARN
TO EXPLORE AND DISCOVER
THE WIDE WORLD THAT
AWAITS ALL OF US

Table of Contents

Foreword

Art Imitates Life
— By Jane Austen

It is with no small degree of gratitude and astonishment that I write this foreword for *To Pemberley and Beyond*. When first I took up my pen to chronicle the events of Hertfordshire, Derbyshire, and beyond, I could scarce have imagined that the lives of my dear friends and acquaintances would inspire such a curiosity in readers near and far. Yet here we are, and I find myself both humbled and delighted to see their world expanded upon, enriched by the voices of those I so affectionately depicted.

I owe an immeasurable debt to my dear friends—the Bennets, the Darcys, the Bingleys, and indeed all those whose lives were so lovingly shared in Pride and Prejudice. Their gracious willingness to allow me to capture their joys, trials, and triumphs has created a narrative that has resonated with so many hearts. It is now a joy to witness the same friends take to these pages, lending their own voices to guide the curious traveller through the locales that shaped their lives.

To the readers of this travel guide, I extend my sincerest thanks. It is your enthusiasm for the world depicted in Pride and Prejudice that has inspired this collection of essays, observations, and advice from the very individuals who lived these stories. Through their words, you will come to know not only the beauty of England's countryside but also the spirit of its people.

I encourage you to visit Hertfordshire and Derbyshire, to walk the paths of Longbourn, Netherfield, and Pemberley, and to immerse yourself in the lively assemblies, tranquil gardens, and charming towns that define our England. May you find, as I did, that these places are far more than mere settings—they are reflections of the characters and the lives that inhabit them.

As you turn these pages, may you hear the voices of my beloved Elizabeth Bennet Darcy, Fitzwilliam Darcy, and their friends as clearly as I did when first I captured their stories. Their perspectives, humour, and wisdom bring this guide to life, transforming it from a mere manual into an invitation to journey into a world of elegance, warmth, and discovery.

With heartfelt thanks to the publishers and contributors, and with the fondest hopes for all who read this volume, I remain,

Yours most sincerely,

Jane Austen

Prologues

The Story Within the Story:
How Jane Austen Saw Us All
— By Elizabeth Bennet Darcy

&

When my dear friend and confidante Miss Jane Austen first approached me with her unexpected request to chronicle the events of our lives, I confess, I was both amused and bewildered. To record our little world—the drawing rooms, assemblies, country paths, and occasional missteps—seemed, at first blush, an exercise in folly. Who, after all, would find interest in our Hertfordshire routines, our Derbyshire estates, or even the rather tumultuous engagements of our family and acquaintances? Yet, Jane assured me, with a quiet conviction that only she possesses, that there was a story to be told—a tale of pride, prejudice, and a stubborn pursuit of understanding.

How little I suspected that her lovingly-crafted manuscript would travel beyond the genteel parlors of England, into the hands of readers near and far. But here we are, and I find myself adapting to the peculiar reality that Longbourn, Netherfield, and, most prominently, Pemberley, have become destinations of fascination for visitors who tread eagerly in our footsteps.

Miss Austen, ever perceptive and keen, saw a narrative thread that none of us had dared to examine. She took our moments—some mundane, others spirited—and wove them into a story brimming with life, humour, and poignancy. It is both humbling and astonishing to see ourselves thus presented: my dearest sister Jane, so tender and serene; Mr. Darcy, misunderstood but steadfast; my mother, ever delightful in her singularity; and even Lydia, whose reckless vivacity finds a charm of its own under Jane's pen.

It is often said that art imitates life, and in Miss Austen's case, this adage proves doubly true. Her rendering of our lives, while shaped by the narrative demands of her craft, remains an astonishingly faithful portrait of our true selves. Yet, what I find most remarkable is not merely the accuracy of her observations but her ability to uncover meaning and connection in moments we scarcely noticed. A ball becomes a battleground of wit; a country walk transforms into a revelation of character. She captured not only the events but the unspoken truths that lay beneath them, weaving a tapestry as rich and varied as life itself.

The events, as they unfolded, were often as unexpected and vivid as Jane portrayed them. I did indeed walk miles across muddy fields to visit my sister at Netherfield, to the consternation of Mr. Darcy. And yes, my father's library did serve as a refuge when my mother's matchmaking enthusiasm became insupportable. Such details, which might seem trivial to the uninitiated, were transformed by Miss Austen into moments of universal humour and insight. It is humbling, indeed, to see our everyday lives elevated into something akin to art—a reflection of humanity itself, in all its folly, passion, and charm.

The publishers, Quincy Christian Alexander & Celestial Publishing Co., deserve no small measure of credit for their approach to the creation of *To Pemberley and Beyond*. From the outset, they promised that each contributor's voice would remain true, our singular perspectives preserved in all their vivacity and distinct flavour. They wisely chose not to impose the rigid conventions of the typical travel guide upon us, recognizing that the strength of this collection lay in its diversity of voices. Instead of a dull procession of facts and directions, they invited us to share the stories and sentiments that make our homes and lives worth exploring.

This decision has made all the difference. Lady Catherine's steadfast pronouncements on propriety stand in stark contrast to Lydia Wickham's effervescent recounting of her adventures, while my father's dry humour is worlds apart from Mrs. Bennet's effusive enthusiasm. Yet, it is precisely this variety that lends the guide its vitality, much as the colourful array of characters in Miss Austen's novel brings this world to life. Each contributor, unshackled from the constraints of convention, speaks with a voice as distinct and authentic as their character. As travellers read these pages, I hope they will come to see not only the places we inhabit but the people who bring them to life—each with their own perspective, their own story, their own truth.

In allowing us to speak authentically, the publishers have ensured that the guide is more than a mere manual for navigating the English countryside. It is, instead, a living document—a reflection of our lives, as artful and as imperfect as the world it seeks to portray. And in that, it becomes not only a resource for travellers but a document to the enduring power of individual voices and the shared humanity that unites us all. May those who read these pages, and perhaps tread the same paths we walk, find themselves not only informed but inspired by the spirit in which they were written.

It is with no small measure of gratitude that we welcome this newfound interest in our world. If our stories inspire reflection, amusement, or even a desire to visit the charming corners of England we call home, we can only be thankful. And to Jane Austen, whose pen captured what our hearts could scarcely articulate, we owe an eternal debt. She saw not only what was, but what could be—what pride might yield to understanding, what prejudice might give way to love.

And so, dear travellers, I bid you welcome. May your journey through our countryside bring you joy, insight, and perhaps even a touch of the unexpected. But be wary: while the lanes and estates may guide your steps, it is the people you meet along the way who will shape your story most.

With sincere regards,

Elizabeth Bennet Darcy

Opening Pemberley to the World
— By Fitzwilliam Darcy, Esq.

It is with a profound sense of humility and astonishment that I contribute these reflections for To Pemberley and Beyond. The notion that my personal affairs—once guarded with an impenetrable reserve—have become a source of fascination to the public is a reality I never anticipated. That strangers would be curious about my family, my home, and even the missteps I have taken along life's path leaves me, even now, both perplexed and deeply grateful.

The publication of Miss Austen's narrative brought to light matters I once considered too personal for public scrutiny. Yet, in her capable hands, these stories have become more than mere tales; they are lessons in understanding and reconciliation, in the humbling of pride and the overcoming of prejudice. Though I was at first mortified to see my private reflections exposed, I have come to appreciate how Miss Austen's pen has inspired readers to see beyond the surface of events, to uncover the humanity that connects us all.

Pemberley, my home and sanctuary, has always been dear to me—not merely as an estate, but as a reflection of duty, family, and continuity. To know that it now serves as a point of interest for travellers is both an honour and a challenge. Meeting new visitors has not always come naturally to me; I have long struggled with the openness that such encounters require. Yet, to my surprise, I have found great joy in these moments. Hearing the stories of others, learning about their lives, and seeing Pemberley through fresh eyes have enriched my days in ways I could not have foreseen.

I owe an enduring debt of gratitude to those who have stood by me. My wife, Elizabeth, whose wit and vivacity have brightened every corner of my life; my sister, Georgiana, whose gentle spirit continues to inspire me; and my dear friends, the Bingleys, who have taught me the value of cheerfulness and amiable simplicity. To my extended family and acquaintances—yes, even those whose flaws have tested my patience—I owe much of my growth and understanding. Their presence in my life has been a constant reminder that our connections to one another are what make life truly meaningful.

To those who read this guide and venture forth into the England Miss Austen so beautifully chronicled, I extend a warm invitation to visit Pemberley. Stroll through its wooded paths, linger by the sparkling waters of its stream, and share in the quiet majesty of the land I am privileged to steward. In doing so, you will not only come to know Pemberley but also the spirit of Derbyshire itself—a region as noble and enduring as its rolling hills and ancient forests.

Beyond Pemberley, I encourage you to explore the wonders of Hertfordshire, with its lively market towns and pastoral charm; Kent, with its stately homes and traditions; and the bustling vibrancy of London. Each region holds its own treasures, shaped as much by its people as by its landscape. For it is the people who breathe life into these places—each with their own narratives, joys, and challenges.

In extending this invitation, I hope to encourage the same spirit of discovery that has transformed my own life. May you find joy in new connections, wisdom in unfamiliar perspectives, and beauty in the simple act of exploring. Whether you come to Pemberley or any other corner of England, may your journey be as enlightening and rewarding as the one I have been fortunate enough to undertake.

With the warmest regards and deepest gratitude,

Fitzwilliam Darcy

Introduction
— By the Publisher

I t is with great pride and satisfaction that we present *To Pemberley and Beyond: A Traveller's Guide to England by the Bennets, Darcys, and Their Many Friends.*

This extraordinary volume is no ordinary travel guidebook; rather, it is a collection of essays, reflections, and advice penned by the extraordinary individuals whose lives have gained recognition and admiration thanks to Miss Jane Austen's celebrated novel, Pride and Prejudice, published nary one year ago. The remarkable success of Miss Austen's work has introduced readers across the nation—and indeed far beyond our British shores—to the landscapes, society, and peculiarities of life in Regency England.

What makes this volume truly unique is that it has been written by none other than the individuals so artfully captured in Pride and Prejudice themselves, whose perspectives bring unmatched authenticity and charm to its pages. Each contributor brings their own distinctive voice and insights to this volume, making it a rich and varied companion for those wishing to explore England's towns, villages, and countryside so vividly portrayed by the illustrious Miss Austen.

We, the publishers, have taken the bold step of inviting these now-renowned contributors to share their thoughts and experiences, offering a rich and well-rounded exploration of life in the countryside, metropolitan London, and other locales of note. This remarkable collection of voices provides not only practical guidance for travellers but also a vibrant tapestry of perspectives on English society and culture. From the rustic charms of Hertfordshire to the stately grandeur of Derbyshire, this guide invites readers to explore England through the eyes of its most memorable inhabitants.

Elizabeth Bennet Darcy provides thoughtful observations that will inspire readers to see the English countryside not only for its beauty but for its potential as a place of learning, growth, and progress. Fitzwilliam Darcy, Esq. writes with dignity and care about the responsibilities of stewardship, sharing his admiration for the land and the people who call it home. Jane Bennet Bingley reflects on the joy and tranquillity of life at Netherfield that will surely charm all who read it. Charles Bingley writes with infectious enthusiasm about the delights of hosting visitors and the pleasures of country society.

Mrs. Bennet, whose affection for her daughters is evident in every word, recounts their weddings in vivid detail, celebrating the happiness and prosperity each union has brought. Mr. Bennet shares his own observations with a quiet wisdom that offers readers a glimpse into the perspective of a gentleman who knows his family and community well. Lydia Bennet Wickham shares her reflections on social gatherings and the art of conversation. George Wickham offers an eye-opening account of his travels across the land, highlighting the charm of England's towns and inns he has experienced as a gentleman.

Other contributors include Mary Bennet, whose thoughtful essay on intellectual pursuits encourages readers to seek self-improvement and reflection even amidst their travels, and Kitty Bennet, who brings a fresh and vibrant perspective to the world of fashion and social trends. The Gardiners, always perceptive and discerning, provide practical advice for travellers, drawing on their own journeys to illuminate the joys of discovery and the value of meaningful connections. Caroline Bingley, with her impeccable taste and keen eye for detail, shares her expertise on style and society, offering readers a guide to refinement that is as instructive as it is elegant.

No travel guide to the English countryside would be complete without the insights of Lady Catherine de Bourgh, whose authoritative voice imparts a wealth of knowledge on proper decorum and the significance of tradition. Her nephew, Colonel Fitzwilliam, provides a fascinating account of military life in Brighton, offering readers a glimpse into the discipline and camaraderie of the militia. Mr. Collins, ever diligent in his efforts, contributes a detailed and appreciative essay on the grandeur of Rosings Park, a subject he approaches with the utmost respect and admiration, and shares his learned insights on numerous other topics of import.

Together, these voices create a tapestry of life in today's England, weaving together personal reflections, practical advice, and vivid descriptions of the places and customs that define this remarkable countryside. Whether you are drawn to the elegance of Pemberley, the vibrancy of Meryton, or the allure of Brighton, *To Pemberley and Beyond* promises to be an indispensable guide for anyone seeking to explore our glorious England in this year of our Lord 1813. Each contributor has brought their own perspective to this work, and it is the publisher's hope that their words will inspire, inform, and delight readers from near and far.

We have included numerous snippets of Jane Austen's prose from Pride and Prejudice throughout this guide to help place each contributor's perspective in context of the events so illustriously chronicled by Miss Austen.

With sincere thanks to our contributors and to Miss Austen, whose pen first brought these illustrious British citizens into the sunlight,

We remain,
Your devoted publishers,

Quincy Christian Alexander & Celestial Publishing Co., London
1813

Before You Arrive: Understanding Britain

England:
A Nation of Tradition, Progress, and Influence

England stands as a nation at the crossroads of tradition and progress, its landscapes, industries, and people reflecting both its ancient heritage and the transformative changes of industry. With a population of approximately 10 million, the country is a dynamic blend of rural charm, burgeoning towns, and expanding cities. It is a land of rolling green pastures, bustling ports, and newly rising factories, embodying both the timeless beauty of its countryside and the modernity of its industries.

Agriculture remains the backbone of the rural economy. The fertile fields of southern England produce abundant crops of wheat, barley, and oats, while sheep farming on the downs and in the north contributes fine wool for England's textile industry. Yet, technological advancements are reshaping the nation, particularly in the Midlands and the North. Cities such as Manchester, Leeds, and Birmingham have become centres of textile manufacturing, metalworking, and innovation, driven by steam power and mechanized looms. Coal mining in Yorkshire and Durham, along with iron production in the West Midlands, fuels these industries and supports the growing demand for goods at home and abroad.

England's port cities—London, Liverpool, and Bristol among them—are thriving hubs of trade and commerce. London, the capital, is the heart of governance, finance, and culture, home to landmarks like Westminster Abbey, St. Paul's Cathedral, and the bustling docks along the River Thames. Liverpool connects England to its colonies and trading partners, while Bristol serves as a gateway for goods ranging from sugar and tobacco to manufactured textiles.

On the world stage, England is a dominant force. England and its allies continue to defend against the French Empire under Napoleon Bonaparte, with battles fought across Europe, the Mediterranean, and even the Americas. The Royal Navy, the pride of England, ensures control of the seas, enabling the island nation to blockade France, protect its colonies, and maintain its critical role in global trade. England's armies, often in coalition with other European powers, are actively engaged in campaigns on the Iberian Peninsula, where the Duke of Wellington is leading British forces against the French.

In addition to its military efforts, England's influence extends to its far-reaching empire. From the sugar plantations of the Caribbean to the tea and spice trade of India, England's colonial holdings are integral to its economy and global stature. These connections also bring wealth and cultural exchanges, though they are not without their controversies and challenges.

Domestically, England is governed by King George III, though his declining health has resulted in the Regency Act of 1811, placing his eldest son, George, Prince Regent, at the helm of the nation. England is a nation of contrasts—rural yet industrial, traditional yet forward-looking, local in its customs yet global in its influence. It offers visitors the chance to experience the enduring charm of its countryside, the vibrancy of its towns and cities, and the indomitable spirit of a country leading the world.

KING GEORGE THE THIRD, BY THE GRACE OF GOD,
OF THE UNITED KINGDOM OF GREAT BRITAIN
AND IRELAND KING, DEFENDER OF THE FAITH.

The Natural Order:
Observing Rank and Propriety in Civilized Life
— By Lady Catherine de Bourgh

"'Lady Catherine is a very respectable, sensible woman indeed,' added Charlotte, 'and a most attentive neighbour.'

'Very true, my dear, that is exactly what I say,' Mr. Collins added. 'She is the sort of woman whom one cannot regard with too much deference.'"

In an age where civilization stands as the pinnacle of human achievement, it is essential that the pillars of proper decorum and social distinction be upheld with unwavering commitment. It is not merely a matter of personal conduct but a testament to the refinement and superiority of our society. As a woman of high rank and experience, it falls to me to enlighten those who may, through no fault of their own, lack the guidance and understanding necessary to navigate the complex expectations of English society. It is my hope that this essay will provide some insight into the essential principles of decorum, ensuring that propriety and civility are maintained at all times.

To begin, one must understand that the foundation of civilized society is the recognition and observance of rank. It is not enough to merely acknowledge one's own station; one must also exhibit proper deference to those above and maintain a suitable distance from those below. The distinctions of rank and class are not arbitrary but rather divinely ordained, a natural order that ensures the stability and harmony of society. To ignore or blur these distinctions is to invite chaos and vulgarity, two qualities which have no place among respectable people.

For ladies, the observance of decorum begins with one's appearance. A proper lady must always dress in a manner befitting her station, avoiding both ostentation and carelessness. Her attire should reflect her refinement, with fabrics of the finest quality and accessories chosen with care. Simplicity is no excuse for slovenliness, just as extravagance must never tip into vulgarity. The elegance of a lady's dress is a reflection of her character, and to dress inappropriately is to betray a lack of understanding or respect for her position in society.

Equally important is a lady's behaviour in public. Whether attending an assembly, taking a turn about the room, or making a morning call, she must conduct herself with dignity and grace. Loud or excessive laughter, animated gesturing, or any display of undue familiarity is entirely unbecoming. A proper lady speaks with measured tones, her conversation marked by wit and intelligence but never by impropriety or over-familiarity. It is her duty to elevate those around her, guiding the conversation to topics of refinement and intellectual interest rather than descending into gossip or trivialities.

The matter of private decorum is equally significant. Within the home, a lady must be a model of civility and hospitality, treating her guests with courtesy while maintaining her authority as mistress of the house. Her servants must be managed with firmness but also fairness, for the smooth running of a household is a reflection of her capabilities. A proper lady does not indulge in idle complaints or petty grievances; instead, she conducts herself with a calm assurance that inspires respect and admiration.

One of the most egregious breaches of decorum, and one which I feel compelled to address, is the unfortunate trend of unsuitable alliances. A lady of good breeding must never condescend to form attachments with individuals of inferior rank or fortune. Such unions are not only a betrayal of one's family and station but also a disservice to society at large. The mixing of classes undermines the natural order, leading to a dilution of refinement and an erosion of the very standards that distinguish the civilized from the uncivilized. It is the duty of every lady to consider not only her own inclinations but also the expectations and well-being of her family and community.

In this regard, I must caution against the mistaken notion that love alone is a sufficient basis for marriage. While affection is not to be discounted, it must be tempered by reason and guided by a sense of duty. A proper marriage is one that unites families of equal standing, ensuring the preservation of rank and the advancement of mutual interests. To act otherwise is to indulge in selfishness and folly, with consequences that extend far beyond the individuals involved.

Another crucial aspect of decorum is the art of conversation. A proper lady must be well-read and informed, capable of discussing literature, politics, and the arts with intelligence and poise. At the same time, she must avoid any display of arrogance or affectation, for humility is a virtue that enhances even the most distinguished of characters. In the presence of her superiors, she must listen with deference, offering her opinions only when invited to do so. In the company of her equals, she must strive to be agreeable without sacrificing her dignity. And in her dealings with those of inferior rank, she must exhibit a gracious condescension, providing guidance without belittling.

In all things, a lady must strive to maintain the balance between modesty and self-assurance, elegance and simplicity, authority and kindness. It is a delicate art, one that requires constant vigilance and a keen understanding of one's place in the world. Those who master it will find themselves admired and respected, their influence extending far beyond their immediate circle.

As I conclude this essay, I must emphasize that the principles of decorum are not merely rules to be followed but a reflection of one's character and values. To live a life of propriety and refinement is to honour not only oneself but also the society to which one belongs. It is my hope that these observations will provide guidance and inspiration to those who seek to conduct themselves with the grace and dignity befitting a proper lady.

How to Host a Proper Ball
— By Mrs. Bennet

"Oh! my dear Mr. Bennet," Mrs. Bennet said as she entered the room, "we have had a most delightful evening, a most excellent ball. I wish you had been there."

There is no greater opportunity for a family to elevate its social standing than by hosting a grand ball or gala. A well-executed event brings together the finest members of society, provides an occasion for the daughters of the house to showcase their charms, and creates lasting impressions that may lead to prosperous matches. As a lady of experience, I am delighted to share my advice on hosting a ball that will be remembered as the grandest in the Netherfield area.

The invitations must be written on the finest parchment, ideally embossed with a crest or monogram that suggests family prestige. Never settle for plain paper; it would imply a lack of refinement. Each missive should include flowing language, emphasizing the elegance of the occasion, such as:

"The Bennet family cordially invites you to an evening of unparalleled gaiety and merriment at Longbourn Hall."

It is vital to ensure that every eligible gentleman in the area receives an invitation, regardless of prior acquaintance. How else can our daughters secure the attention they deserve?

The drawing room and ballroom must be transformed into a spectacle. Hire the finest decorators—or, better yet, supervise the arrangements personally to ensure perfection. Garlands of fresh flowers should adorn every surface, even if it means importing blooms from London. Roses, lilies, and hothouse exotics such as orchids create an impression of good taste.

Do not neglect the lighting. Chandeliers must be polished to a dazzling gleam, and additional candelabras should be placed in every corner. Nothing flatters a young lady's complexion more than the soft glow of candlelight. What is a ball if not an occasion to shine?

The orchestra must consist of no fewer than six musicians, preferably from London. Local fiddlers simply will not do for a proper ball. A harpsichord is essential, as are violins and a flute. A trumpeter adds grandeur, though some may consider it excessive. I once heard of a family who hired a quartet and were laughed at for their stinginess. Such humiliation must be avoided at all costs. The music program should include a variety of dances—reels, cotillions, and minuets—to keep the guests entertained. A spirited country dance is a must for encouraging interaction among the young people.

The success of any ball depends heavily on the refreshments, as they demonstrate the host's generosity and good taste. A grand table, laden with delicacies, must dominate the dining room. Roast meats, pies, tarts, and jellies are staples. Do not forget an enormous trifle as the centrepiece; the more layers, the better! For drinks, ensure an ample supply of wine, punch, and ratafia. Lemonade should be available for the young ladies. Do not, under any circumstances, run out of champagne, as it is a mark of poor planning and lack of foresight.

The hostess and her daughters must dress to impress. Silk, satin, and muslin gowns with intricate embroidery or lace trimmings are non-negotiable. Matching gloves and fans are essential, as are tasteful but striking pieces of jewellery. I firmly believe that a little extravagance goes a long way in capturing the attention of eligible gentlemen. If possible, hire a hairdresser to create elaborate coiffures adorned with pearls or fresh flowers. A bonnet is unsuitable for such an occasion, but a delicate tiara or jewelled comb adds the perfect finishing touch.

The guest list must include families of good standing, particularly those with eligible sons. Invite neighbouring gentry, regardless of whether they are friends or rivals; the presence of notable figures adds prestige to the gathering. Care must also be taken to ensure a sufficient number of young men to partner the ladies. A poor ratio of gentlemen to ladies is a grave social faux pas and must be avoided. If necessary, invite officers from the local militia, as they add liveliness to the dance floor and potential suitors.

First impressions are paramount. Guests should be greeted at the door by liveried footmen and escorted into the drawing room. The hostess must position herself prominently to welcome each arrival warmly, ensuring every guest feels honoured. An opportune moment for introductions must be created. It is vital to draw attention to one's daughters without appearing too eager. This delicate balance will ensure they are noticed without the appearance of desperation.

ENGLISH HALF EVENING DRESS

While dancing is the centrepiece of any ball, additional entertainments demonstrate creativity and thoughtfulness. Consider hiring a magician or a poet to provide diversion between sets. Small games of chance, such as cards or whist, offer a quieter option for those who prefer not to dance. Some may undoubtedly dismiss these amusements as frivolous, but I assure you, they are precisely the kind of touch that leaves an impression on the guests.

The hostess must circulate throughout the evening, ensuring that every guest is attended to and no one is left standing awkwardly in a corner. It is imperative to introduce gentlemen and ladies who may benefit from each other's company. Subtle matchmaking is the hallmark of a skilled hostess, though discretion must always be observed.

As the evening draws to a close, the hostess must thank her guests warmly and express a desire to see them again soon. Small parting gifts, such as sachets of lavender or candied almonds, leave a favourable impression and ensure the event is remembered fondly.

Hosting a ball is no small undertaking, but the rewards are immeasurable. A successful gala elevates the host's reputation, strengthens social ties, and provides opportunities for advantageous connections. I maintain that every detail contributes to the overall splendour of the occasion. After all, one never knows when a wealthy gentleman may attend and find himself utterly captivated.

And so, my dear readers, I urge you to embrace the art of hosting with enthusiasm and diligence. Spare no expense, for a well-executed ball is a masterpiece of elegance and opportunity, ensuring that the honour and ambitions of your family are upheld for generations to come.

The Art of Chaperonage:
Ensuring Propriety and Protecting Honour
— By Mrs. Gardiner

LADIES AT A GARDEN PARTY

"The Gardiners stayed only one night at Longbourn, and set off the next morning with Elizabeth in pursuit of novelty and amusement. One enjoyment was certain--that of suitableness as companions; a suitableness which comprehended health and temper to bear inconveniences--cheerfulness to enhance every pleasure--and affection and intelligence, which might supply it among themselves if there were disappointments abroad."

In an age where a family's reputation is a delicate treasure, entrusted to the behaviour of its young ladies, the role of a chaperone is both essential and sacred. It is a duty not merely of supervision but of guidance, ensuring that the actions and interactions of the young reflect decorum, propriety, and respectability. As a woman who has observed both the perils and triumphs of social engagements, I offer this essay as a guide for those who, like myself, find themselves entrusted with this noble responsibility.

A female chaperone is the sentinel of propriety, ever vigilant to ensure that the young ladies in her care are shielded from situations that might compromise their reputation or invite scandal. However, her role extends beyond mere supervision. She is also a mentor, offering wisdom and counsel to help her charges navigate the complexities of social life with grace and confidence. A chaperone must balance watchfulness with subtlety, ensuring that her presence is felt without being overbearing. The young lady must feel her freedom respected, even as she is quietly protected from impropriety. It is a delicate art, requiring discernment, tact, and unwavering commitment.

To fulfil this role effectively, a chaperone must embody certain virtues and skills.

The ability to discern character and intentions is paramount. A chaperone must quickly identify unsuitable company and guide her charge away from potentially compromising situations.

While a chaperone must be observant, she must also be discreet. Publicly chastising a young lady or drawing attention to her missteps can do as much harm as the impropriety itself.

A chaperone must be unwavering in her principles, gently but resolutely guiding her charge in the right direction, even in the face of youthful obstinacy.

Young ladies must feel that their chaperone is an ally, not an oppressor. A compassionate approach fosters trust and encourages openness, making it easier to offer guidance.

A chaperone must accompany her charge to balls, assemblies, and other social gatherings, ensuring that she is introduced to respectable company and avoids the notice of those with questionable intentions. She should subtly observe the interactions of her charge, stepping in if a gentleman becomes too familiar or a conversation turns inappropriate.

While the young lady must ultimately decide her own future, a chaperone can play a vital role in guiding her toward suitable suitors. She must assess the character, fortune, and intentions of potential matches, offering advice without imposing her own preferences. Courtship is a time of heightened sensitivity, where even the appearance of impropriety can jeopardize a young lady's reputation. The chaperone must oversee meetings, ensuring that they occur in appropriate settings and under her watchful eye. She must also counsel her charge on the importance of modesty, prudence, and decorum. When young ladies travel, whether to visit family or attend social gatherings, the presence of a chaperone is indispensable. It is her duty to ensure that accommodations are respectable, interactions with strangers are limited, and all journeys are undertaken with safety and propriety.

In society, appearances are everything. A chaperone must be mindful of how her charge's actions are perceived, ensuring that they do not become fodder for malicious gossip. Even innocent indiscretions, such as spending too much time in the company of a single gentleman, can lead to damaging speculation.

The role of a chaperone is not without its difficulties. Young ladies, particularly those spirited and independent in nature, may bristle at the constraints of supervision. In such cases, it is crucial to frame guidance not as an imposition but as a form of care and respect. A chaperone must also manage her own feelings, avoiding partiality or undue interference in the young lady's choices, while still maintaining her commitment to propriety. Another challenge lies in balancing trust and oversight. A chaperone must allow the young lady some measure of autonomy, fostering her ability to make sound decisions, while still remaining close enough to intervene if necessary.

While the responsibilities of a chaperone are weighty, the rewards are equally profound. There is great satisfaction in seeing a young lady blossom under one's guidance, navigating social life with confidence and grace. To know that one has played a part in securing her happiness, whether through a felicitous match or the preservation of her reputation, is a reward that far outweighs the effort. Moreover, the chaperone herself gains respect and admiration for her dedication to this noble task. In fulfilling her duty, she upholds not only the honour of the young lady's family but also the values of society itself.

The role of a female chaperone is a sacred trust, requiring vigilance, wisdom, and a deep sense of duty. In an age where a single misstep can irreparably harm a family's reputation, the chaperone serves as both protector and guide, ensuring that young ladies navigate the complexities of social life with propriety and grace. Let those who undertake this role do so with the seriousness it deserves, for their efforts safeguard not only the honour of their charges but also the values that bind society together. And to the young ladies under their care, let them see their chaperones not as impediments to their freedom but as allies in their journey toward a future of respectability, happiness, and success.

A Visitor's Guide to Understanding English Humour
— By Elizabeth Bennet Darcy

"Mr. Bennet, how can you abuse your own children in such a way? You take delight in vexing me. You have no compassion on my poor nerves."

"You mistake me, my dear. I have a high respect for your nerves. They are my old friends. I have heard you mention them with consideration these twenty years at least."

If you are visiting England for the first time, you may quickly discover that humour is one of our most cherished pastimes, woven into the very fabric of our conversations. It is not, however, always immediately apparent to the untrained ear, for English humour often takes the form of quiet subtlety rather than loud exuberance. This, I assure you, is not due to a lack of joy or liveliness but rather a preference for wit that rewards attentiveness and reflection.

The essence of English humour lies in its understated nature, where a well-placed remark or a slight change in tone can transform the simplest statement into something deeply amusing. Take, for instance, our fondness for irony. To say something entirely opposite to what one means, while maintaining a tone of complete sincerity, is an art that many Englishmen and women practice with pride. Consider the often-discussed English weather, a topic so inexhaustible that it has become a humourist's delight. On a particularly rainy day, a gentleman might remark, "What a glorious summer we are having," and though his tone is entirely serious, a spark of mischief lies within the statement. To those attuned to this gentle irony, such remarks are a shared joke, a moment of levity drawn from the everyday.

This shared understanding is at the heart of English humour. It thrives in the connections between people, where unspoken recognition turns a dry comment into something delightful. Our humour is not designed to draw attention to itself; rather, it invites a smile, a knowing glance, or even the faintest chuckle from those who understand its subtlety. For this reason, I encourage visitors to observe closely and listen carefully, for much of our wit lies in the unsaid as much as the spoken.

One of the great joys of English humour is how it reflects the world around us. Whether teasing the quirks of a dear acquaintance or acknowledging the peculiarities of society at large, our humour is often born from an affectionate awareness of human nature. It is not cruel or cutting but instead aims to bring people together through recognition and shared experience. Miss Jane Austen, whose work has so captured the attention of readers far and wide, has a remarkable talent for this very skill, illuminating the absurdities of life with a lightness that leaves us all nodding and smiling in agreement.

English humour also knows no boundaries of station or setting. You may hear it in the lively chatter of a ball, in the quiet murmur of a village green, or even at the breakfast table, where a wry comment about the toast might elicit a laugh. A clever hostess, for example, can steer the tone of an entire evening with a few choice remarks, just as a shopkeeper might brighten a transaction with a witty observation. This universality is one of its most charming qualities, for it ensures that humour is something shared, no matter where you find yourself.

To newcomers, understanding English humour may feel like solving a puzzle, but I assure you the effort is well worth it. The key is patience and a willingness to see beyond the surface of a remark. Often, what appears to be a simple statement contains layers of meaning that reward closer inspection. And while our humour may not always announce itself loudly, it welcomes those who are curious enough to seek it out.

Of course, humour is best enjoyed in good company. Whether over tea, during a dance, or while strolling the countryside, the opportunity to exchange a jest or share a laugh brings people together in a way that nothing else can. One need not have an endless repertoire of clever remarks to join in; often, the simplest observations, spoken with sincerity and a touch of warmth, are the most endearing.

For those visiting England, I encourage you to embrace the playfulness of English humour, to delight in the quirks of conversation and the joy of shared laughter. Listen for the irony, watch for the twinkle in an eye, and allow yourself to be drawn into the world of subtlety and wit that defines so much of our daily interactions. Humour here is not about performance or applause but about connection, a quiet understanding that brings smiles to even the rainiest of days.

And should you find yourself amidst a gathering, do not hesitate to engage. Ask about the weather, comment on the tea, or simply enjoy the interplay of voices around you. You may find that humour here, like the countryside itself, reveals its beauty gradually, offering new delights with each passing moment.

For those willing to see it, English humour is as much a part of our landscape as the rolling hills or the ancient oaks. It is a source of light and warmth, a reminder that even in life's challenges, there is always room for laughter and understanding. May it bring as much joy to you as it does to us, and may your journey through England be filled with smiles and sparkling conversation.

The Rhythm of a Country Day:
A Guide to Social Customs
— By Jane Bennet Bingley

BREAKFAST

"Mr. Bennet was among the earliest of those who waited on Mr. Bingley. He had always intended to visit him, though to the last always assuring his wife that he should not go; and till the evening after the visit was paid, she had no knowledge of it."

Life in the English countryside, though often described as tranquil, follows a rhythm as structured and steady as the ticking of a fine clock. For those unacquainted with our ways, it may seem puzzling at first to determine when and how one should engage in the social customs of the day. There are unspoken rules—some dictated by politeness, others by practicality—that govern everything from a neighbourly call to the arrangement of meals. Allow me to offer a guide to help any visitor navigate the ebb and flow of our daily life with ease.

The day begins, naturally, with morning, though one must not assume this is an hour for social activity. Mornings in the countryside are typically reserved for private matters, whether they involve correspondence, reading, or household management. Should you need to communicate with a neighbour, it is best done by post, for a visit before noon would be considered unseemly unless it is a matter of urgency. The morning also offers time for quiet walks or, in some cases, light exercise on horseback, but these pursuits are best undertaken without expectation of encountering company.

As the clock approaches noon, the social world begins to stir. The hour from noon to two o'clock is often reserved for visits, provided the nature of the call is brief and businesslike. Whether you seek to convey an invitation, deliver a message, or simply exchange pleasantries, this is the window in which such endeavours are most welcome. It is important to note that visits at this hour are not intended for prolonged conversation or refreshment; they are formal, courteous, and conducted with a sense of efficiency.

Luncheon, a light meal served around one o'clock, is by no means universal in country households. Some families adhere to a simpler schedule, reserving their appetite for the main meal later in the day, while others enjoy a small repast of bread, cold meats, or fruit. As a visitor, it is wise to inquire whether luncheon is customary before assuming you will partake in it. If offered, accept it graciously, as it is often a gesture of hospitality rather than a grand occasion.

The afternoon, following luncheon, is a time for leisure and sociability. This is the hour for strolls through the garden, calls on neighbours of longer duration, or, for the more ambitious, a drive to a nearby town. Calls made in the afternoon are less formal than those earlier in the day and may involve tea or light refreshment if your host is particularly obliging. It is customary to bring a token of goodwill—perhaps flowers from your garden or a small gift from your travels—as a gesture of appreciation for your host's hospitality.

Tea, that most quintessential of English customs, is typically served between four and five o'clock, though the precise hour may vary from household to household. This is a convivial affair, offering an opportunity for conversation and relaxation. A well-prepared tea table will include an array of offerings: scones, biscuits, or cakes, accompanied by clotted cream, jams, and, of course, an excellent pot of tea. Guests are expected to partake with enthusiasm but not excess, and conversation should remain lively yet polite. It is during tea that one might engage in the delightful art of gentle gossip, though always with an air of discretion.

Dinner, the grandest meal of the day, is served at varying hours depending on the household's standing and traditions. In simpler homes, it may be as early as four or five o'clock, while in more fashionable circles, it could be delayed until eight or even later. Dinner is a formal event, often involving multiple courses and a well-curated array of wines. Guests are expected to arrive punctually, dressed in their finest attire, and prepared to engage in spirited conversation. The seating arrangement, carefully orchestrated by the host or hostess, often reflects social standing and relationships, so it is wise to approach your designated seat with gratitude rather than complaint.

Following dinner, the company may retire to the drawing room for further conversation, music, or games. This is the hour when friendships are deepened, alliances are forged, and the day's events are discussed with warmth and reflection. Gentlemen may linger in the dining room for port and politics, but they are expected to rejoin the ladies before too long, lest they be accused of neglect.

As the evening winds down, it is customary for guests to take their leave at a reasonable hour, expressing their gratitude to the host with a sincere farewell. Those staying overnight, whether due to distance or the lateness of the hour, should be mindful of the household's rhythms the following morning, rising promptly and taking care not to impose.

In all these customs, the underlying principle is one of thoughtfulness—toward one's hosts, neighbours, and the broader community. To call at the appropriate hour, to arrive punctually, to engage in conversation with charm and civility—these are the hallmarks of a well-mannered visitor. And, perhaps most importantly, to respect the rhythm of the day is to honour the quiet dignity of life in the English countryside.

To those unfamiliar with these customs, I assure you they are less rigid than they appear and more delightful in practice than in description. They are the threads that weave our social fabric, lending structure to our interactions and ensuring that, even in a world as expansive as the countryside, no one feels forgotten or out of place. Whether you are here for a day, a season, or a lifetime, I invite you to embrace the rhythm of our lives and discover the joy it brings.

From Brighton to Bliss:
A Bride's Grand Adventure
— By Lydia Wickham

BRIGHTON

"Only think of its being three months," Lydia cried, "since I went away; it seems but a fortnight I declare; and yet there have been things enough happened in the time. Good gracious! when I went away, I am sure I had no more idea of being married till I came back again! though I thought it would be very good fun if I was."

How thrilling it is to travel, especially with a husband as handsome and charming as my dear Mr. Wickham! I can hardly believe my fortune in becoming Mrs. Wickham, and I am positively bursting with delight to share the details of our journey—from the lively streets of to our new home in Tyne and Wear. Every stop along the way was an adventure, filled with bustling inns, delightful food, and the knowledge that I am now married to the most dashing man in all of England.

We began, of course, in Brighton, the very pinnacle of excitement and society. Brighton is the perfect place for a young lady to meet officers, dance, and enjoy the sea air, and I must say, I made quite a splash there before my marriage. The town is simply alive with activity! Every evening seemed to hold a ball, and every day was an opportunity to promenade along the shore. The inns were lively, filled with people coming and going, and the chatter of fashionable company was music to my ears. Mr. Wickham and I dined at a cozy little inn near the water, where the seafood was so fresh that I declared it the best meal I had ever had—until the next one, of course.

VIEW OF THE BATHING ROOMS AND PIER

From Brighton, we travelled to Epsom, a charming little town with its own distinct character. Epsom has a quieter air than Brighton, but it is no less delightful. We stayed at an inn called The Gilded Horse, run by a jolly innkeeper named Mr. Thornton and his wife, a cheerful woman who insisted on serving us the largest meat pies I have ever seen. The rooms were cozy, with little lace curtains at the windows and a fireplace that crackled merrily all evening. Mr. Wickham told me tales of his adventures in the militia as we sat by the fire, and I could not help but feel that life was more splendid than I had ever dreamed.

Next, we made our way to Clapham, a bustling suburb just outside of London. The inn here, The Rose and Crown, was not as grand as I had hoped, but it had a charm all its own. The innkeeper's daughter, a shy girl named Emily, seemed positively in awe of my bonnet (a new one with crimson ribbons, which I wore for the first time that day). I told her all about my recent marriage, and she looked as though she could hardly believe her ears. The food was simple but satisfying, and the ale—which Mr. Wickham enjoyed immensely—was said to be the best in the area.

And then, oh, the excitement of Cheapside! London itself is a marvel, but Cheapside has a vibrancy all its own. The streets are alive with vendors calling out their wares, and the shops are filled with every imaginable delight—ribbons, gloves, bonnets, and trinkets to make any young lady's heart flutter. We stayed at The Silver Bell, a quaint little inn with a charming garden in the back. The breakfast there was a feast: fresh rolls, butter, and the sweetest marmalade I have ever tasted. I must admit, I spent quite a bit of time admiring myself in the mirror of our room, as the morning light made my new gown look positively radiant.

From London, we travelled to Barnet, a quieter town that felt like a lovely pause before the final leg of our journey. The inn, The Traveller's Rest, was warm and welcoming, with the kindest staff I have ever encountered. The innkeeper, Mr. Jameson, insisted on telling us stories of all the travellers who had stayed there, and I listened with wide-eyed fascination. The countryside around Barnet was beautiful, and we took a walk together, with Mr. Wickham promising to buy me a new ribbon in the village shop—a promise he kept, of course.

BATHING MACHINES

And now, we are settled in Tyne and Wear, where my husband is stationed with the militia. Our new home is charming, with a view of the rolling countryside that I find quite romantic. The town itself is lively enough, with plenty of shops and places to visit, though I confess I sometimes long for the excitement of Brighton. Still, I am content, for I am Mrs. Wickham, and there is no greater title in the world. We often dine at The Red Fox, a local inn with the most delightful roast beef and a pudding that I can never resist. The townspeople seem very impressed by Mr. Wickham's uniform, and I, of course, am more than happy to tell them about our journey and our happy life together.

A COACH AND FOUR TRAVELING THE ROADS

My journey from Brighton to Tyne and Wear was nothing short of magical. Each town brought its own charm, and every inn we stayed at had its own little delights. I feel as though I have stepped into a dream, one where I am not only adored by my husband but also admired by everyone we meet. I can only hope that every young lady is as fortunate as I have been, though, of course, there can only be one Mrs. Wickham!

Travelling Across England:
The Turnpike Gatekeepers
— By Mr. Bennet

THE ENGLISH TURNPIKE

"After making every possible enquiry on that side London, Colonel F. came on into Hertfordshire, anxiously renewing them at all the turnpikes, and at the inns in Barnet and Hatfield, but without any success, no such people had been seen to pass through."

To those unacquainted with the peculiarities of English travel, it is my solemn duty to prepare you for an unavoidable reality: the Turnpike Gatekeeper. These hardy souls, stationed at intervals along our nation's great roads, are as much fixtures of the journey as the milestones and the ruts. To pass through their gates is both an art and a trial, requiring patience, fortitude, and occasionally—though it pains me to admit it—a silver coin or two.

The Turnpike Gatekeeper is a peculiar breed, a union of surly authority and stubborn practicality. Their task, as they will not hesitate to remind you, is to ensure the smooth operation and maintenance of the roads by collecting tolls from travellers. However, as with all individuals vested with even the smallest measure of power, they sometimes wield their authority with a zeal that can try the temper of the calmest soul.

TRAVELLING IN COMFORT

To approach a Turnpike Gatekeeper, one must first prepare oneself for the encounter. Ensure that your carriage or horse is brought to a complete stop, for nothing irritates these sentinels of the road more than a traveller who exhibits impatience. A hearty "Good day, sir" or "Good day, madam," delivered with a tone of respectful indifference, is often sufficient to disarm their natural suspicion. Do not, under any circumstances, attempt to hurry them in their duties; for if you do, you will find your progress delayed by questions and inspections that might otherwise have been dispensed with.

Payment, of course, is the crux of the transaction, and here one must tread carefully. The toll required is typically posted on a weather-beaten board by the gate, but the figures are sometimes obscured by the ravages of time and weather. Inquire politely if you are uncertain of the amount, and do not grumble if the fee appears excessive. To do so is to invite a lecture on the importance of road maintenance, delivered in tones that could scour the varnish from your carriage.

It is wise to keep a supply of small coins readily accessible. Offering a large denomination note or expecting the gatekeeper to provide change is an invitation to delay, if not outright irritation. Should you lack the exact amount, a humble apology coupled with a cheerful countenance may work wonders. These individuals are, after all, human, and even the sternest gatekeeper can be softened by a display of good humour.

TRAVELLER STOP IN TOWN

For those travelling with passengers or cargo, be prepared for inquiries. The Turnpike Gatekeeper is a keen observer of both people and goods, and they delight in ferreting out inconsistencies. If you are carrying a particularly large or curious load, it is best to declare it openly rather than wait for them to question you. Transparency, though tedious, will often speed your journey.

Occasionally, one encounters a gatekeeper who takes their duties with excessive seriousness. These individuals are to be treated with the utmost caution. Responding to their officiousness with sarcasm or impatience will only prolong your suffering. Instead, adopt an air of solemnity that mirrors their own, and they will often relent in their zeal, satisfied that they have impressed you with the gravity of their position.

Let me assure you, however, that not all Turnpike Gatekeepers are cut from the same cloth. Some, though rare, are endowed with a surprising civility and may even engage in pleasant conversation, should time and circumstances permit. It is during such encounters that one is reminded that even the most seemingly intractable individual may harbour a spark of kindness beneath their gruff exterior.

When I had opportunity to travel across the towns and villages of England, I encountered a host of such gatekeepers, each more colourful than the last. In Hertford, there was old Mr. Potts, whose weathered visage and perpetual squint suggested he had long since grown accustomed to scrutinizing travellers with suspicion. His bark was far worse than his bite, and a compliment to his gate's pristine upkeep won me an uncharacteristically cheerful farewell.

In Stamford, I met Mrs. Trewitt, a rare female gatekeeper who commanded her station with all the authority of a general inspecting her troops. Her inquiries into my business were as sharp as her gaze, but a half-penny over the toll seemed to thaw her frosty demeanour, and she even wished me "safe travels" as I departed.

The turnpike at Grantham was presided over by young Tom Fincher, whose enthusiasm for his duties was rivalled only by his enthusiasm for gossip. He regaled me with tales of every traveller who had passed through in the last month, sparing no detail, until I was forced to plead urgent business to escape his chatter.

At Leicester, the gatekeeper Mr. Crowley proved a dour and taciturn fellow. His gate was the most meticulously maintained I had ever seen, yet his silence rendered the transaction almost theatrical. A simple nod concluded our business, and I continued my journey with a sense of relief.

JUMPING THE TOLL GATE

Further north, in Nottingham, I encountered Mr. Blenkinsop, who fancied himself something of a philosopher. He inquired not only after my toll but also my thoughts on the state of the nation's roads, offering his own unsolicited views at great length. A nod and a coin were my only contributions to the debate.

In Derby, Mrs. Wainscott surprised me with her hospitality, offering me a cup of tea while she counted my coins with maddening slowness. Her kindness, though well-meant, delayed me nearly as much as the more officious gatekeepers I had met.

Each gatekeeper, in their own way, contributed to the peculiar charm of my journey. While some were gruff, others loquacious, and a few surprisingly kind, all were united in their steadfast guardianship of their gates. And so, dear traveller, I leave you with this: should your path lead you through England's turnpikes, regard the gatekeepers not as obstacles but as characters in the great tapestry of our nation's roads.

Baked in Greatness: England's Culinary Triumph
— By Mr. Collins, Rector of Hunsford

THE ENGLISH SCONE

"The dinner too in its turn was highly admired; and Mr. Collins begged to know to which of his fair cousins, the excellence of its cookery was owing. But here he was set right by Mrs. Bennet, who assured him with some asperity that they were very well able to keep a good cook, and that her daughters had nothing to do in the kitchen. He begged pardon for having displeased her. In a softened tone she declared herself not at all offended; but he continued to apologise for about a quarter of an hour."

It is with the deepest sense of duty and propriety that I, William Collins, take this opportunity to extol one of England's most venerable creations: the scone. Were I to neglect such an essay in favour of lesser gastronomic pursuits, I should be remiss in fulfilling my obligation to celebrate that which elevates our national identity above all others. Indeed, to write of the English scone is not merely to address the palate, but to honour the very hand of Providence, which has surely guided our kingdom's culinary traditions to their zenith.

The scone, in its noble simplicity, stands as an examplar to the virtues of restraint and refinement. Unlike the French croissant, which, with its excessive butter and frivolous folds, seeks to dazzle the senses, or the Greek baklava, so indulgently sweet as to invite gluttony, the scone embodies temperance. Whether plain or enriched with the judicious addition of currants or raisins, the scone never stoops to excess. On the contrary, the scone reflects the uprightness of English character.

Let us consider the scone in its proper setting: upon a well-laid tea table, accompanied by clotted cream, preserves, and a pot of fine Darjeeling tea. Such an arrangement is not merely a repast but an emblem of civility, a moment wherein the virtues of hospitality and good breeding are most perfectly displayed. To partake of a scone is to engage in an act of communal decency, to break bread—so to speak—with one's companions in an atmosphere of decorum and grace. How could one imagine a Frenchman or a Greek partaking of such an occasion without veering into some lamentable display of frivolity or ostentation?

As a man of the cloth, I am compelled to draw parallels between the English scone and the sacred loaves of Scripture. In its plainest form, the scone is reminiscent of unleavened bread, which the Israelites themselves were commanded to consume during their flight from Egypt. Yet how much more glorious is the English scone, leavened with the lightest hand and baked to golden perfection. Truly, this culinary marvel must be counted among the blessings of a God-fearing nation, bestowed upon us as a mark of divine favour.

Allow me also to reflect upon the moral dimension of the scone, which offers sustenance without courting temptation. The French croissant, for all its layers and artifice, whispers of vanity, while the rich, honeyed baklava of Greece might well serve as a metaphor for overindulgence. The scone, by contrast, is an invitation to moderation. It is substantial without being excessive, flavourful without being cloying—a balance that mirrors the virtues of the English spirit itself. How fitting that it should be a staple of our tea tables, which are, after all, gatherings of propriety and reflection, not frivolity and excess.

Though I am no traveller, my authority on foreign pastries is nevertheless informed. I have heard of other confections sampled by those in my circles—and, if I may say so, from the discerning palate of Lady Catherine de Bourgh herself—that no other nation has managed to produce a baked good of such moral clarity and wholesome appeal. That I have never personally tasted the croissant, the baklava, or any other foreign confection, far from undermining my opinion, only underscores my wisdom in avoiding that which might corrupt both body and soul.

Let all who read these words take to heart the unparalleled virtues of the English scone. May it be revered not merely as a culinary delight but as a symbol of all that is right and good in our blessed land. And should any visitor to our shores wish to partake of this treasure, let them seek it with proper humility and gratitude, acknowledging that in its golden crust lies a reflection of England's greatness.

The Gentleman's Compass:
Enjoying England with Decorum
-- By George Wickham

REGIMENTAL SOLDIERS

"Mr. Wickham was the happy man towards whom almost every female eye was turned, and Elizabeth was the happy woman by whom he finally seated himself; and the agreeable manner in which he immediately fell into conversation, though it was only on its being a wet night, and on the probability of a rainy season, made her feel that the commonest, dullest, most thread-bare topic might be rendered interesting by the skill of the speaker."

A gentleman in the company of his military brethren bears not only the distinction of his uniform but also the responsibility of upholding the honour and propriety of his comrades. In my years of service with His Majesty's militia, I have always striven to be that guiding force—a beacon of reason and temperance amidst the whirl of excitement and temptation that our fair towns and cities offer. Whether in the quiet streets of Meryton, the refined elegance of Bath, or the bustling energy of London, I have made it my solemn duty to ensure that my fellow officers conduct themselves with the utmost decorum, always acting in a manner befitting gentlemen of our rank.

SALOON AT THE MARINE PAVILION

Allow me, then, to recount some of my travels through these locales, not as tales of frivolity but as instructive examples of how one might navigate the many delights of England while remaining steadfast in one's principles. Though the towns I have visited teem with opportunities for merriment, I have ever been vigilant in reminding my companions of their responsibilities and steering them away from any lapses in judgment.

Let us begin with Meryton, a town whose unassuming charm might lull a less discerning visitor into complacency. While stationed there, I took it upon myself to foster goodwill between the officers and the local populace, particularly the young ladies and their families, who were naturally eager to make our acquaintance. It was no small task, I assure you, to ensure that my comrades behaved with the utmost respect and courtesy in their interactions. I recall one instance when a young officer, newly arrived and overly enthusiastic, sought to monopolize the attention of a certain Miss Mary King, a lady of considerable fortune and refinement. Sensing that his eagerness might be misconstrued, I intervened with great tact, gently redirecting his attentions and ensuring that Miss King was treated with the dignity she deserved.

The assembly rooms of Meryton, though modest, provided a welcome opportunity for polite society to mingle. I confess, I did enjoy the occasional dance, but only in the spirit of camaraderie and good manners. My wife, Lydia, who was then only a charming acquaintance, will tell you that I often encouraged others to partake in the lively reels and cotillions while I observed from the sidelines, ever mindful of my role as a steadying influence. It was not uncommon for younger officers to become overly animated during these gatherings, and I took it upon myself to ensure that the wine flowed sparingly and the conversations remained suitably genteel.

From Meryton, let us turn to Bath, that glittering jewel of refinement and leisure. Bath, with its soothing waters, has long been a destination for those seeking both health and amusement. While others may have found the card tables at the Assembly Rooms or the convivial atmosphere of the Pump Room too great a temptation, I prided myself on maintaining a measured approach. It was not uncommon for my comrades to become overly engrossed in the games of chance that Bath offers, but I always ensured that stakes remained reasonable and that no gentleman placed his honour—or his pocketbook—at undue risk.

On one occasion, a particularly headstrong young officer found himself in a game that had grown rather too spirited. Seeing the danger, I intervened with a well-timed word of caution, reminding him of his duty to his regiment and his family. He later thanked me profusely, acknowledging that my intervention had saved him from a regrettable loss. Such moments, though demanding, are the very essence of camaraderie and leadership, and I was glad to be of service.

The social life of Bath, of course, extends beyond the gaming tables. The promenades along the Royal Crescent and the afternoons spent sipping tea in the Pump Room provide ample opportunity for conversation and connection. I made it my mission to ensure that my comrades presented themselves as gentlemen of distinction, encouraging thoughtful discussions on literature, politics, and the arts rather than idle gossip or flirtation. My wife, Lydia, often reminds me of how she admired my ability to steer such conversations with charm and wit, and I can only hope that my efforts were as effective as she claims.

FEASTING IN THE SALOON

Finally, we arrive at London, that bustling metropolis where opportunity and temptation lie side by side. London, as you must know, is a city that demands vigilance, particularly for those unaccustomed to its pace and complexity. While others may have been drawn to its theatres, gaming houses, and taverns with reckless abandon, I took it upon myself to act as a guide and protector to my comrades, ensuring that their forays into the city were both enjoyable and above reproach.

The theatres of Drury Lane, with their dazzling performances and lively crowds, were a particular favourite of the regiment. While some officers might have been tempted to linger too long in the company of actresses or to overindulge in the refreshments served during intermission, I always reminded them of the importance of restraint. My role, as I saw it, was to ensure that their enjoyment of the evening did not come at the expense of their dignity.

The same can be said of London's famed gaming houses, where the allure of cards and dice is matched only by the thrill of victory—or the sting of defeat. While I cannot deny the pleasure of a well-played hand, I always approached such activities with a sense of responsibility, setting an example for my comrades by knowing when to step away and encouraging them to do the same. My wife, Lydia, often boasts of my "remarkable self-control," and while I am far too modest to agree, I can only hope that my actions speak for themselves.

Whether in the quiet charm of Meryton, the refined elegance of Bath, or the vibrant energy of London, I have always sought to balance enjoyment with responsibility, to embrace the opportunities for diversion while maintaining the honour and decorum expected of a gentleman and an officer. It is my hope that this account will serve as a guide to others, reminding them that true enjoyment lies not in excess but in the steady, thoughtful appreciation of all that England has to offer.

Now, I find myself stationed in the bustling region of Tyne and Wear, where I reside in wedded bliss. Our modest yet cheerful home is a sanctuary of domestic tranquillity, a refuge where I can momentarily set aside the weight of my responsibilities and enjoy the many charms of married life. Lydia is, of course, the very picture of youthful energy and delight, filling our home with laughter and good spirits. It pains me deeply, then, that my duties as a responsible officer require me to leave her company so often, for the men under my command seem to require near-constant guidance to maintain their sense of decorum while enjoying the lively diversions that Tyne and Wear has to offer.

At great personal expense, I have taken it upon myself to act as a chaperone of sorts for my fellow soldiers during their evening excursions. Though it is far from my preference to abandon the quiet comforts of my home, I recognize the importance of my presence in ensuring their good behaviour. Tyne and Wear, as you may know, offers a variety of amusements—taverns, music halls, and other establishments designed to entertain—and it would be all too easy for young and impressionable men to stray from the path of propriety without a steady hand to guide them. Thus, I endure the tedium of these outings, dragging myself from one establishment to another, all in the noble pursuit of keeping my comrades in line.

How often do I sit in a corner of some bustling tavern, casting a watchful eye over the proceedings while lamenting my absence from home! Lydia frequently protests my departures, imploring me to remain with her and enjoy a quiet evening by the fire, but my sense of duty will not allow it. She, of course, is most understanding of my responsibilities.

It is a burden I bear with reluctance but also with pride, knowing that my efforts contribute to the honour and reputation of our regiment. The men, I might add, are grateful for my vigilance, often expressing their admiration for my steadying influence and commitment to their welfare. I only wish that such endeavours were not quite so exhausting, but such is the price of responsibility.

Of course, as you follow my account, you might detect a hint of self-sacrifice that I wear with great humility. Surely, nothing could please me more than remaining at home with my dear wife, but alas, duty calls, and I, ever the responsible and devoted officer, must answer. Let it never be said that Mr. Wickham shirked his responsibilities to his regiment—or his fellow man. A man must make sacrifices, after all, and though I bear mine with a heavy heart, I do so with the utmost determination to maintain the highest standards of conduct among those in my charge.

Hertfordshire County:
A Picture of Rural Charm

Hertfordshire, a county of moderate size located just north of London, offers visitors a blend of rural charm and convenient proximity to the capital. With a population of approximately 110,000, it is a thriving region characterized by its pastoral landscapes, bustling market towns, and historic estates.

The county is renowned for its rich agricultural output, with fertile soil supporting the cultivation of wheat, barley, and oats. Sheep grazing and cattle farming are also common, contributing to the local economy and ensuring a steady supply of goods to London markets. Hertfordshire's position along major coaching routes, such as the Great North Road, facilitates trade and travel, making its market towns, including Hertford and St. Albans, lively hubs of activity. Hertford, the county town, boasts a longstanding charter and serves as a centre of governance and commerce.

For the historically inclined, St. Albans is a highlight not to be missed. This ancient town, named for Britain's first Christian martyr, offers visitors a glimpse of Roman Verulamium, with ruins of the old city walls and a theatre still visible. St. Albans Abbey, a majestic medieval cathedral, continues the region's ecclesiastical heritage.

Travelers will find the Hertfordshire countryside dotted with charming villages, each with its own character. The gently rolling hills and tree-lined lanes offer endless opportunities for leisurely exploration. Estates such as Hatfield House, the grand Jacobean home of the Cecil family, stand as monuments to the county's aristocratic history. Built in 1611, Hatfield House is steeped in Tudor and Stuart history, having been the childhood home of Queen Elizabeth I.

Hertfordshire combines the tranquillity of the English countryside with the vibrant commerce and culture of its towns, making it a delightful destination for visitors seeking both history and natural beauty.

Meryton: A Lively Market Town

THE MARKET AT MERYTON

Meryton, is a charming market town nestled in the rolling countryside of Hertfordshire, with a population of approximately 1,500. It serves as a central hub for the surrounding villages, drawing farmers, tradespeople, and gentry alike to its weekly market and social gatherings.

The town's primary industry is agriculture, reflecting the fertile lands of Hertfordshire, which produce abundant crops of wheat, barley, and oats. Meryton's market square comes alive each week with stalls offering fresh produce, livestock, and everyday goods, fostering a lively exchange of commerce and conversation. The town's proximity to major coaching routes also makes it a convenient stop for travellers heading to London or other southern destinations.

Meryton's historic charm is enhanced by its parish church, a modest but well-kept building at the heart of the community, and several fine inns that provide comfortable lodging and hearty meals. The George Inn, with its cheerful atmosphere and warm fires, is particularly noted for its hospitality.

Though small in size, Meryton is not lacking in social vibrancy. Assemblies held in its local room bring together residents and visitors for evenings of dancing and conversation, and the arrival of a regiment of militia often adds a dash of excitement to local life.

Oakham Mount, a modest yet picturesque hill near the market town of Meryton, offers visitors a tranquil escape into the natural beauty of Hertfordshire. Though not imposing in height, the mount provides a commanding view of the surrounding countryside, with rolling fields, hedgerows, and distant church spires creating a tapestry of pastoral charm. It is a favoured spot for both locals and travellers seeking quiet reflection or a leisurely stroll.

For those seeking a picturesque and convivial stop on their travels, Meryton offers a perfect blend of rustic charm and lively community spirit. Its markets, inns, and social opportunities make it a delightful addition to any journey through Hertfordshire.

Visiting Longbourn
— By Elizabeth Bennet Darcy

LONGBOURNE

"Mr. Bennet's property consisted almost entirely in an estate of two thousand a year, which, unfortunately for his daughters, was entailed in default of heirs male, on a distant relation; and their mother's fortune, though ample for her situation in life, could but ill supply the deficiency of his."

If by chance or design your path meanders through the picturesque countryside of Hertfordshire, I invite you to pause at Longbourn, my cherished family home. While it may lack the grandeur of a Pemberley or the polish of Netherfield, Longbourn embodies the essence of warmth, family, and the quiet beauty of the English countryside. It is a house filled with stories, laughter, and life, nestled amidst fields and gardens that mirror the gentle rhythms of the land. Allow me to guide you through this beloved home, where the heart is as vibrant as the hearth.

The journey to Longbourn is a delight for the senses, offering a prelude to the charm that awaits. The roads leading here are a tapestry of countryside simplicity, bordered by hedgerows that hum with life. Depending on the season, the air may carry the heady scent of wildflowers, the earthy aroma of freshly turned soil, or the crisp tang of autumn leaves.

As you approach, you will notice fields stretching wide and open, their gentle undulations an attestation to the enduring partnership between the land and its caretakers. Livestock graze serenely, their presence a reminder of the steadiness of rural life. There is a timeless quality to these scenes, as if the very landscape conspires to slow your pace and invite reflection.

Travellers should note that the roads, while charming, are not without their quirks. Rain may render them muddy, and dry spells leave them dusty, but these minor inconveniences are easily forgotten amidst the splendour of the journey. Whether you come on horseback or on foot, the countryside rewards every step with its quiet beauty.

THE DRAWING ROOM

Upon entering Longbourn, you will find yourself drawn to its library, a room that radiates the quiet dignity of its most frequent occupant, my father, Mr. Bennet. It is a space of calm contemplation, where the cares of the world seem to fade in the presence of well-loved books and the gentle rustle of turning pages.

The library is not grand, but it is thoughtfully curated. Shelves are lined with volumes spanning history, literature, and the occasional indulgent romance, each book bearing the marks of frequent use. The room itself is cozy, with a sturdy writing desk by the window and a chair that seems to have been shaped by years of contented reading. For my father, it is a sanctuary, a place where he can indulge his insatiable curiosity in peace. For me, it has been a retreat, a space to lose myself in a story or to ponder the world beyond the confines of Hertfordshire. Should you seek intelligent conversation, you will find it here—though be prepared, for my father's humour is as quick as it is clever.

Longbourn's dining room is more than a place to eat; it has been the heart of our family's daily rituals. The sturdy oak table has borne witness to countless meals, from simple breakfasts to celebratory feasts, always accompanied by the lively conversation that defines our household. Here, the Bennet family gathers not only to share food but to exchange ideas, stories, and sometimes spirited opinions. My mother, Mrs. Bennet, presides over these meals with an enthusiasm that can be both endearing and exhausting. Her greatest delight is ensuring that her daughters' futures are well provided for, and her hopes and plans often spill forth in lively detail over the course of a meal. The food, prepared with care and tradition, reflects the bounty of the land. Roasts and puddings, hearty soups, and fresh-baked bread fill the air with enticing aromas. It is a setting where laughter is as abundant as the dishes on the table, and where each member of the family contributes their unique flavour to the conversation.

Longbourn's garden is a place of simple but profound beauty, where the natural world flourishes in harmony with human care. The front garden greets visitors with vibrant blooms—roses, daisies, and hollyhocks—that brighten the path and fill the air with their fragrance. This colourful display is evidence of the gardener's skill and the occasional enthusiastic efforts of my sisters. Beyond the ornamental beds lies a kitchen garden, its rows of vegetables and herbs a source of both sustenance and pride. The garden is practical yet picturesque, a place where the cycles of planting and harvesting unfold with quiet regularity. The orchard, tucked away at the garden's edge, offers a different kind of charm. Fruit trees stand in graceful rows, their branches heavy with apples and pears in the autumn. This secluded spot is a favourite retreat of mine, a place to reflect, dream, or simply enjoy the gentle rustling of leaves in the breeze.

The drawing room at Longbourn is where the family comes together to unwind and enjoy each other's company. The furnishings, though simple, are comfortable and well-loved, exhibit years of happy use. The room is warmed by a fireplace that crackles cheerfully on colder evenings, casting a golden glow over its occupants. It is here that my sisters and I spent many an evening. Lydia and Kitty often chatter about the latest gossip from Meryton, their youthful exuberance filling the room with laughter. Mary, ever earnest, may play a piece on the pianoforte, her music a backdrop to the lively conversations that swirl around her. My mother ensures that every guest feels welcome, while my father observes the proceedings with his customary mix of amusement and affection. The drawing room is not a place of grandeur but of genuine warmth. It is a space where relationships are strengthened, joys are shared, and the occasional disagreement is softened by the enduring bonds of family.

LONGBOURN'S SIMPLE COMFORTS

Longbourn may not have the opulence of a great estate, but its true wealth lies in its character. It is a home filled with love, laughter, and a deep connection to the land and each other. Every room, every corner, carries the imprint of those who live here, making it a place that feels alive in every sense. For those seeking a glimpse of life in the English countryside, Longbourn offers an experience that is as enriching as it is endearing. It is a house where the doors are always open, where every visitor is welcomed with warmth and sincerity, and where the rhythms of life unfold with a quiet but profound beauty.

Should your travels bring you near, I encourage you to visit. Longbourn will not dazzle you with marble halls or gilded ceilings, but it will embrace you with a charm that lingers in the heart long after you have departed.

Visiting Netherfield Park
— By Charles Bingley

NETHERFIELD PARK

"Mr. Bingley had not been of age two years, when he was tempted by an accidental recommendation to look at Netherfield House. He did look at it and into it for half an hour, was pleased with the situation and the principal rooms, satisfied with what the owner said in its praise, and took it immediately."

Welcome to Netherfield Park! It is with great delight that I, Charles Bingley, extend this introduction to my home—though it is rented, it feels nothing short of entirely my own. And, if I may be so bold, much of its charm has only grown since I began sharing it with my dear wife, Jane. We live here blissfully, surrounded by beauty, warmth, and the cheer of Hertfordshire's verdant countryside. For those unfamiliar with English estates or the splendour of country living, I hope this account will inspire you to visit Netherfield and experience its wonders firsthand.

Netherfield Park is nestled in a neighbourhood as welcoming as it is picturesque. The journey here is a pleasure in itself, with roads that wind through rolling fields and pass by cheerful villages like Meryton. Along the way, you will encounter hedgerows alive with birdsong, wildflowers waving in the breeze, and perhaps even the occasional rabbit darting across your path.

The people of Hertfordshire are as pleasant as the scenery, and I dare say my neighbours have made me feel more at home here than in any other place I have known. There is a sense of community that imbues every interaction, whether at a lively assembly or a quiet market day. It is impossible not to feel buoyed by the spirit of the land and its people.

It is no exaggeration to say the gardens of Netherfield are a jewel among the estate's many treasures. Vibrant and meticulously maintained, they are a tribute to the skill and dedication of the gardeners. Jane and I often take our morning walks along the gravel paths, marvelling at the variety of blooms that grace the flowerbeds. Roses of every hue cascade along trellises, their fragrance perfuming the air, while tulips and dahlias lend their bright colours to the formal beds. Boxwood hedges frame each section with precision, leading the eye naturally to the centrepiece: a grand fountain whose gentle cascade of water soothes the soul. Beyond the ornamental gardens lies a kitchen garden, a quieter but no less impressive space where rows of vegetables and herbs thrive. This productive corner of the estate ensures that our table is always graced with the freshest produce. The grounds also boast a charming orchard, where Jane and I have spent many a lazy afternoon under the shade of fruit-laden trees. In the distance, a small woodland beckons those seeking solitude or adventure. It is a landscape that invites exploration, offering a new delight at every turn.

The drawing room at Netherfield is the very heart of our home. It is here that we gather with friends and family, where the sound of laughter mingles with the crackle of the fire. The room is spacious yet cozy, with tall windows that flood the space with light during the day and frame views of the gardens outside. The furnishings are elegant but never ostentatious, chosen for their comfort as much as their beauty. Jane has a particular knack for arranging the room in a way that feels both inviting and refined. A pianoforte graces one corner, often brought to life by Jane's graceful hands or the talents of our guests. In the evenings, the drawing room comes alive with conversation, games, and music. It is a space where time seems to slow, allowing us to savour the simple joys of companionship and the warmth of home.

If the drawing room is where the heart gathers, the dining room is where it celebrates. This room, with its grand table and polished silver, is the stage for meals that are as much about fellowship as they are about sustenance. Jane takes great pleasure in planning the menus, working closely with the kitchen staff to ensure that every dish is both delicious and beautifully presented. From hearty roasts to delicate pastries, the meals at Netherfield reflect the bounty of the land and the care of those who prepare them. The atmosphere is warm and inviting, perfect for both intimate dinners and lively gatherings.

THE DRAWING ROOM

Netherfield's charms extend far beyond its main rooms. The library, though modest in size, is well-stocked with books that Jane and I both enjoy. It is a quiet retreat where one can lose themselves in a story or ponder the wider world. The bedrooms, too, are delightful. Each is decorated with care, offering comfort and a touch of luxury. Our own room overlooks the gardens, and waking to the sight of sunlight streaming through the trees is a daily joy. The conservatory, a recent addition, is a favourite spot for us on rainy days. Filled with exotic plants and flooded with light, it is a space where one can feel close to nature even when the weather is less than agreeable.

Living at Netherfield has been a dream, one made all the sweeter by sharing it with Jane. Her presence brings warmth and grace to every corner of the house, transforming it from a mere residence into a true home. Together, we have filled these rooms with love, laughter, and the promise of a bright future. We are often joined by friends and family, whose visits add to the lively spirit of Netherfield. Jane's sister Elizabeth, and her husband, Mr. Darcy, provide a steady and thoughtful counterpoint to my own exuberance.

Netherfield Park is more than a house; it is a living, breathing validation to the joys of country life. It is a place where nature and human care work in harmony, where the beauty of the land is matched only by the warmth of the home. For those who long for peace, it offers tranquillity. For those who seek connection, it provides the perfect setting for friendship and family. And for those who simply wish to wander, it is a world of delights waiting to be discovered.

A Guided Walk from Longbourn to Netherfield Park

"Elizabeth continued her walk alone, crossing field after field at a quick pace, jumping over stiles and springing over puddles with impatient activity, and finding herself at last within view of the house, with weary ancles, dirty stockings, and a face glowing with the warmth of exercise."

Distance: Approximately 3 miles

Difficulty: Moderate

Terrain: Varied, with some muddy patches after rain

The walk from Longbourn, the Bennet family home, to Netherfield Park offers an engaging route through the heart of the Hertfordshire countryside. This journey is one that delights the lover of rural England with its scenic views, natural beauty, and occasional challenges. Sturdy footwear is recommended, especially in damp weather.

The walk begins at Longbourn, a comfortably situated house surrounded by neat gardens and enclosed by hedgerows. Departing from the main gate, the path turns onto a country lane bordered by hawthorn and wild roses in season. This initial stretch is gentle and well-trodden, offering views of fields where sheep and cattle graze peacefully.

The Meadow Crossing

After about a mile, the lane gives way to an open meadow, a stretch that may prove the most picturesque yet the most challenging underfoot. In fair weather, the meadow is dotted with wildflowers—daisies, buttercups, and the occasional poppy—and the air hums with the sound of bees and skylarks. However, after recent rain, the ground can become soft and uneven, requiring care to navigate without mishap.

The Stream and Footbridge

Continuing onward, the path descends gently toward a clear, bubbling stream. A wooden footbridge spans the water, a quaint structure weathered by years but sturdy underfoot. This is an excellent spot to pause and take in the surroundings, the tranquil sound of the stream providing a natural symphony. Look for kingfishers darting along the banks, their bright plumage a vivid contrast to the green foliage.

The Woodland Path

Beyond the stream, the path enters a small wood, where the canopy of oak and ash provides shade and shelter. In the spring, bluebells carpet the forest floor, creating a magical atmosphere. This section of the walk is particularly charming, though the ground may be littered with fallen leaves.

The Climb to Netherfield

Exiting the wood, the route ascends a gentle incline, bringing Netherfield Park into view. The house, with its stately stone facade, stands prominently atop a rise, commanding a view of the surrounding countryside. The final approach is along a gravel drive, bordered by a line of lime trees that were likely planted generations ago.

Arrival at Netherfield Park

Upon reaching Netherfield, the traveller is greeted by the house's impressive symmetry and the well-kept lawns that surround it. This walk, though simple in length and design, encapsulates the rural charm of Hertfordshire. It is a route that rewards the walker with natural beauty, the occasional test of endurance, and the satisfaction of arriving at one of the finest estates in the area.

Visiting The Philips House
— By Mrs. Philips

THE PHILIPS HOUSE

"Some of them were to dine with the Philipses the next day, and their aunt promised to make her husband call on Mr. Wickham, and give him an invitation also, if the family from Longbourn would come in the evening. This was agreed to, and Mrs. Philips protested that they would have a nice comfortable noisy game of lottery tickets, and a little bit of hot supper afterwards. The prospect of such delights was very cheering, and they parted in mutual good spirits."

Meryton is a bustling market town, the very heart of the neighbourhood. The roads leading here are well-travelled and lively, bringing all manner of visitors, from local farmers to the officers of the militia. Shops line the main street, offering everything from fine ribbons to the latest fashions, and there is always a hum of conversation and activity.

Our house sits just off the main thoroughfare, close enough to be part of the action but far enough to avoid too much noise. From my window, I can see the comings and goings of neighbours and visitors alike, and it is a rare day when there isn't some bit of news worth sharing. If you value community spirit, you will find no better place than Meryton, where everyone knows everyone—and where everyone's business is everyone's concern (in the most neighbourly of ways, of course).

Now, I won't claim that our grounds rival those of a great estate, but they have their own charm. A small garden frames the front of the house, with neat flowerbeds that I tend to myself. It is no grand affair, but the blooms are cheerful, and in spring, the scent of lavender and roses drifts through the open windows. Behind the house, there is a tidy courtyard where we often gather in fair weather. It is here that I keep a few pots of herbs for the kitchen, along with a small bench where one might sit and enjoy the sunshine. Though modest, the grounds suit our needs perfectly and provide a pleasant bit of green in the midst of the town.

THE PARLOR

The ballroom is the pride of our house and the site of many lively gatherings. While not as grand as the great halls of a true estate, it is spacious enough to accommodate a fine assembly, as it did the night we hosted the Bennet ladies, Mr. Collins, and Mr. Wickham. That evening is one I shall never forget—how splendid it was to see the room alive with music, laughter, and the rustle of fine gowns! The room itself is well-appointed, with polished wooden floors that shone in the candlelight and enough space for dancing. The walls are adorned with simple but tasteful decorations, and the large windows allow the light of the evening sun to filter in before the candles are lit. On the night of a party, the room truly comes alive, filled with the sounds of a lively reel or the murmur of animated conversation. I must confess, I do enjoy being a hostess, and the ballroom is where I feel most in my element. Whether it is a gathering of neighbours or a celebration with family, it is a space that brings people together and fills the house with joy.

The parlour is another favourite space of mine, where I welcome visitors for tea and conversation. It is a cozy room, furnished with comfortable chairs and a well-stocked tea table that is always ready to receive guests. I pride myself on creating a warm and inviting atmosphere, and many an afternoon has been spent here in the company of friends and relations. The dining room is perfectly suited to our needs. The table is always set with care, and the meals served here are comforting. I do enjoy entertaining, and whether it is a simple supper or a more elaborate feast, it is always a pleasure to share our table with others.

My house in Meryton is not a place of grandeur, but it is a place of warmth, laughter, and community. It is a house that welcomes all who enter with open arms, whether they come for a lively ball or a quiet cup of tea. The spirit of our home reflects the spirit of Meryton itself—lively, friendly, and ready for a bit of merriment.

Michaelmas in Hertfordshire:
Observations of the Season
— By Charles Bingley

"Why, my dear, you must know," said Mrs. Bennet. "Mrs. Long says that Netherfield is taken by a young man of large fortune from the north of England; that he came down on Monday in a chaise and four to see the place, and was so much delighted with it that he agreed with Mr. Morris immediately; that he is to take possession before Michaelmas, and some of his servants are to be in the house by the end of next week."

My first journey to Netherfield, arriving as it did at the time of Michaelmas, remains one of the most pleasant and invigorating experiences of my life. There is something about the turning of the season, when the air grows brisk and the leaves catch fire with colon, that fills a man with a renewed sense of purpose. To undertake such a journey in autumn is to feel oneself part of the great adventure of the natural world, and as the carriage rolled along the roads of Hertfordshire, I could not help but marvel at the splendour of the countryside. Though my thoughts naturally turned to the practicalities of taking up residence at Netherfield, my heart was buoyed by the beauty of the landscape and the promise of new beginnings.

The weather, for a journey in late September, was remarkably fine, as though the heavens themselves were inclined to favour my arrival. The sky stretched wide and clear above me, a brilliant blue softened only by the occasional wisp of a cloud. The sun, though gentler than in high summer, still cast a golden warmth over the fields and woods, lending a glow to the world that seemed almost magical. I confess that I spent much of the journey with my head turned toward the window, eager to take in every detail of the scene before me. The air, crisp and invigorating, carried the faint scent of earth and woodsmoke—a fragrance that I have always associated with the comfort of autumn.

The trees, too, seemed to be dressed for the occasion, their leaves turning to shades of gold, amber, and crimson as if to celebrate the season. I found myself thinking, rather fancifully, that the landscape resembled an illustration from one of the adventure stories I enjoyed as a boy, where brave knights or daring explorers embarked upon journeys into enchanted forests. There is a sense of enchantment in the countryside at this time of year, as though the familiar world has been transformed into something extraordinary. Every hedgerow, every path, seemed to invite exploration, and I resolved that once I was settled at Netherfield, I would make it my business to acquaint myself with every corner of the estate and its surroundings.

As we neared Netherfield, the landscape began to take on a more cultivated aspect. The fields were neatly divided by hedgerows, and the occasional glimpse of a distant farmhouse or grazing sheep lent a sense of peace and order to the scene. It struck me that this was precisely the kind of place where a man might find contentment—neither too wild nor too tame, but a perfect balance of natural beauty and human endeavour. I was reminded of a passage from a novel I had read, in which the hero, having endured many trials, comes at last to a haven where he might rest and find happiness. Such a haven, I thought, was Netherfield.

The house itself came into view quite suddenly, its handsome façade framed by tall trees and approached by a long gravel drive. Netherfield had a charm that was immediately apparent. It stood with an air of quiet dignity, as though it had always been there and would always remain, watching over the land it graced. I felt a thrill of anticipation as the carriage drew nearer, for it seemed to me that this house was a place where life might unfold in the most agreeable manner—filled with friends, laughter, and the kind of lively gatherings that I have always enjoyed.

As I stepped out of the carriage and made my way into the house, I could not help but feel that I was embarking on a new chapter of my life. The season of Michaelmas seemed a fitting time for such a beginning. There is something deeply satisfying about arriving at a place where one feels both the promise of the future and the comfort of the present, and I could not have wished for a more auspicious start to my time at Netherfield.

In the days that followed, I made good on my resolution to explore the estate and its surroundings. I walked through the woods, where the sunlight filtered through the leaves in a golden haze, and I wandered along the paths that bordered the fields, delighting in the small discoveries that each turn revealed. There was a pond, its surface reflecting the colours of the trees like a mirror, and a small orchard where the apples hung heavy on the branches. Everywhere I went, I was reminded of the richness of the season and the quiet joy that comes from being part of such a beautiful and harmonious world.

My impressions of that first journey to Netherfield remain vivid to this day, and I often think back on it with gratitude and pleasure. To travel through Hertfordshire in autumn is to be reminded of the simple yet profound pleasures of life. Netherfield has since become a home in every sense of the word, but that first glimpse of it, framed by the colours of Michaelmas, will always hold a special place in my memory.

The Joys of the Season:
Christmas at Longbourn
— By Mrs. Gardiner

"On the following Monday, Mrs. Bennet had the pleasure of receiving her brother and his wife, who came as usual to spend the Christmas at Longbourn. Mr. Gardiner was a sensible, gentleman-like man, greatly superior to his sister, as well by nature as education."

The Christmas season is always a time of great joy and reflection, but there is something particularly heartwarming about spending it at Longbourn, amidst the lively company of the Bennet family. My visit there during the holiday season remains a memory I cherish, not only for the warm reception I received but also for the charming traditions and simple pleasures that made the time so delightful. The season itself, with its frosty mornings and crackling fires, seemed to lend a particular brightness to the household, and I could not help but feel that this time of year brings out the very best in people and places alike.

The weather, though sharp and cold, was invigorating. Frost painted the landscape in delicate patterns, transforming the familiar countryside into something magical. The trees, stripped of their leaves, stood like silent sentinels against the pale sky, while the fields lay in quiet repose beneath a thin veil of frost. The short days and long nights, though often melancholy in other seasons, felt perfectly suited to the coziness of Christmas, when the warmth of home and hearth seems all the more inviting.

At Longbourn, the spirit of the season was evident in every corner of the house. Mrs. Bennet took great pride in ensuring that Christmas was celebrated with proper cheer. The house was adorned with greenery gathered from the surrounding countryside—holly, ivy, and fir branches draped over mantels and wound around banisters, their fresh scent mingling with the aromas of baking and roasting that filled the air. A cheerful fire burned in every grate, and the glow of candlelight added to the atmosphere of warmth and festivity.

The Bennet family's Christmas traditions were as lively and varied as the family itself. The mornings were often spent in bustling activity, with the younger girls—Kitty and Lydia—flitting about with an energy that seemed immune to the cold. Elizabeth and Jane, ever sensible, took charge of the more practical arrangements, ensuring that the household ran smoothly and that every guest felt welcome. There was a particular charm in observing these sisters, each so different in temperament, working together in harmony. I confess that I took great pleasure in lending a hand where I could, for there is no better way to feel part of a family than by sharing in its labours and joys.

The evenings at Longbourn were filled with merriment. There were games and music, with Mary providing a steady supply of solemn airs on the pianoforte, though the more lively tunes seemed to inspire greater enthusiasm among the company. Dancing was, of course, a favourite pastime, and the sight of the Bennet girls twirling about the room, their cheeks flushed with exertion and laughter, was enough to warm even the coldest winter night. Mr. Bennet, though often content to observe from his corner with a wry smile, occasionally joined the fray with a dry remark or a particularly clever turn of phrase that left us all laughing.

One of the most delightful aspects of the holiday was the abundance of good food and drink. Mrs. Bennet had ensured that the table was well supplied with Christmas fare. There were roasts and puddings, mince pies and spiced wines, all prepared with a care that reflected the importance of the occasion. I must admit that I found particular satisfaction in the Christmas pudding, a dish that seems to embody the richness and warmth of the season. It was served flaming, to the delight of all, and accompanied by a cheer that rang through the house.

Outdoors, the season offered its own diversions. The younger members of the family delighted in sledding down the nearby hills, their laughter echoing across the frosty fields. Walks through the countryside were a pleasure, as the beauty of the winter landscape never failed to lift the spirits.

As I reflect on my time at Longbourn during the Christmas season, I am struck by the warmth and generosity that defined the holiday. The Bennet family exemplified the true spirit of Christmas: a spirit of kindness, cheer, and togetherness. It is a time that I shall always remember with fondness, not only for the festivities themselves but for the sense of belonging and joy that permeated every moment. Christmas at Longbourn, with its lively company and simple pleasures, is a reminder of the enduring charm of family and tradition.

Derbyshire County: Gem of the English Countryside

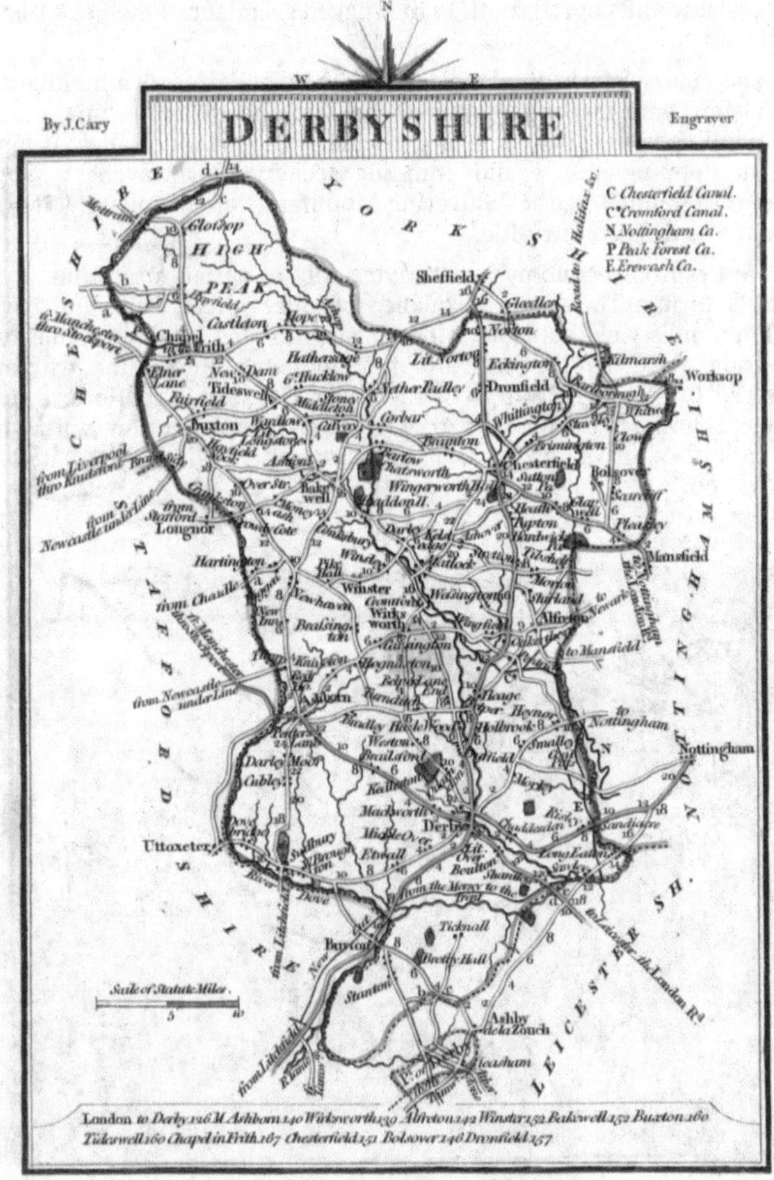

Derbyshire, located in the heart of England, is celebrated for its striking natural beauty and its blend of rural tranquillity and industrious activity. With a population of approximately 140,000 in 1812, the county is known for its diverse landscapes, ranging from the pastoral lowlands in the south to the rugged grandeur of the Peak District in the north.

The Peak District, England's first true upland area, is a highlight for any visitor, with its dramatic limestone dales, heath-covered moorlands, and winding rivers. Dovedale, a particularly picturesque valley, is famed for its stepping stones and stunning scenery. For travellers seeking adventure, Mam Tor, the "Shivering Mountain," offers splendid views of the surrounding countryside.

Derbyshire's economy is a thriving mix of agriculture, mining, and manufacturing. The fertile farmlands produce wheat, oats, and barley, while the hills yield valuable minerals such as lead, coal, and limestone. The county is also at the forefront of the Industrial Revolution, with mills powered by the swift waters of the River Derwent. Cromford, a small village, is home to Sir Richard Arkwright's pioneering cotton mills, which revolutionized textile production and earned the region a reputation for innovation.

EXHIBITION OF WATER COLOURED DRAWINGS

Historically, Derbyshire boasts significant landmarks. Chatsworth House, the opulent seat of the Dukes of Devonshire, is renowned for its splendid architecture and expansive gardens. Haddon Hall, a well-preserved medieval manor, offers a glimpse into England's feudal past. Visitors may also explore the spa town of Buxton, famed for its mineral springs and elegant Georgian Crescent, a fashionable retreat for health and leisure.

Derbyshire combines natural splendour, historical significance, and industrial progress, making it a captivating destination for travellers in search of England's varied charms.

ANCIENT FONT IN ASHOVER CHURCH, DERBYSHIRE

Pemberley: A History
— By Fitzwilliam Darcy, Esq.

PEMBERLEY

"Elizabeth, as they drove along, watched for the first appearance of Pemberley Woods with some perturbation; and when at length they turned in at the lodge, her spirits were in a high flutter. The park was very large, and contained great variety of ground. They entered it in one of its lowest points, and drove for some time through a beautiful wood, stretching over a wide extent. Elizabeth's mind was too full for conversation, but she saw and admired every remarkable spot and point of view. They gradually ascended for half a mile, and then found themselves at the top of a considerable eminence, where the wood ceased, and the eye was instantly caught by Pemberley House, situated on the opposite side of a valley, into which the road with some abruptness wound."

Pemberley, my ancestral estate, is a home which has borne the weight of my family's legacy for many generations. I offer this guide to acquaint you with its history and character, that you might walk its grounds with understanding and appreciation.

Pemberley, situated in the county of Derbyshire, owes its origins to the ambition of my forebear, Sir Everard Darcy, who acquired the land in the late fifteenth century. It was, at that time, a modest property, comprising little more than a manor house surrounded by fertile pastures. Sir Everard, a man of discernment and enterprise, had returned from the tumult of foreign campaigns to seek a quieter pursuit: the cultivation of his estate and the establishment of his family. Legend holds that Sir Everard's foresight led him to commission the first Darcy Library, a modest but respectable collection of legal and theological works, the cornerstone of what would become one of Pemberley's most revered treasures.

Under Sir Everard's careful stewardship, Pemberley grew in both size and reputation. He took great pains to establish strong relations with neighbouring families, believing that unity among the local gentry would ensure prosperity for all. It was during his tenure that the estate's first gardens were laid out, albeit in a style far simpler than the designs one admires today. The emphasis was on practicality: orchards for sustenance, herbs for healing, and a modest flower garden to lend beauty to the surroundings. His vision of Pemberley as a place where family, community, and nature coexisted harmoniously laid the foundation for the estate's enduring legacy.

His son, Sir Percival Darcy, inherited his father's industrious spirit but added to it a touch of grandeur. Inspired by his travels to London and the Continent, Sir Percival undertook a significant expansion of Pemberley House. The original manor was transformed into an elegant residence. Drawing upon the architectural trends of the Elizabethan period, Sir Percival ensured that every addition to the estate reflected both taste and practicality. It is said that he hosted numerous gatherings at Pemberley to foster a sense of camaraderie and mutual support among the gentry of Derbyshire.

In those early days, Pemberley also became known for its fair dealings with its tenants. Sir Percival's wife, Lady Margaret, was a woman of great compassion and foresight. She established the first tenant school on the estate, believing that education was the surest path to self-sufficiency and dignity. This tradition of benevolent oversight has been maintained by each successive generation of the Darcy family, ensuring that Pemberley is not merely a seat of wealth but a community where all who live and work within its bounds can thrive.

The Golden Age of Pemberley

The eighteenth century brought to Pemberley its most celebrated steward, my great-grandfather, Sir Benedict Darcy. A man of lofty ambition tempered by rare good sense, Sir Benedict was instrumental in modernizing the estate. His marriage to Eleanor Montague, a lady of impeccable taste, marked a turning point in Pemberley's aesthetic development. Together, they commissioned Capability Brown himself to redesign the grounds, transforming Pemberley into a place where nature seemed artless yet contrived to delight the senses.

The lake, now one of the estate's most admired features, was expanded under Sir Benedict's guidance, with its banks artfully adorned by groves of oak and willow. Visitors to Pemberley often remark upon the reflection of the great house upon its waters, a sight that has inspired both poets and painters.

My Father's Stewardship

It is with a measure of personal sentiment that I recount the contributions of my own father, George Darcy, a man whose quiet dignity and unshakable integrity set an enduring example. Under his care, the estate flourished, not merely as a repository of wealth but as a haven for those under its protection. George Darcy was a man of singular judgment, and his benevolence extended to the tenants, whose well-being he regarded as inseparable from the prosperity of Pemberley.

My father's marriage to Lady Anne Fitzwilliam, a woman of grace and gentle resolve, brought a warmth to Pemberley's halls. My mother's influence was keenly felt in the drawing rooms, where she curated an atmosphere of refinement without ostentation. Her passing, though it came too soon, left an indelible void, and yet her spirit endures in the tranquil elegance of Pemberley's interiors.

To those who are unacquainted with English customs, I would offer this thought: Pemberley, like Derbyshire itself, is a place where the natural and the cultivated exist in harmony. It is a land of quiet beauty, where the changing seasons are marked not only by the turning of the leaves but by the rhythm of life itself. Autumn brings the golden hues of harvest, winter the sharp clarity of frost, spring the renewal of green, and summer the fullness of bloom. Each season offers its own pleasures, its own reminders of the constancy of time and the cycles of nature.

I hope this account has offered some sense of the place I am fortunate to call home. Pemberley is not merely a house or an estate; it is a living representation of the values of steadiness, harmony, and care.

Visiting Pemberley
— By Georgina Darcy

THE GRAND HALL AT PEMBERLEY

"It was a large, handsome, stone building, standing well on rising ground, and backed by a ridge of high woody hills;--and in front, a stream of some natural importance was swelled into greater, but without any artificial appearance. Its banks were neither formal, nor falsely adorned."

I write with no small degree of trepidation, for I cannot help but feel unequal to the task of describing a place as dear to me as Pemberley. Yet, as I reflect upon the many visitors who have remarked upon its beauty, I am encouraged to hope that even my humble account might convey some sense of its charm and the natural loveliness of Derbyshire that surrounds it. Though I am but seventeen, and shy of the eloquence of more practiced writers, I shall do my best to offer an honest portrait of the home I hold so dear.

Derbyshire itself is a county of unspoiled beauty, with its hills and dales stretching far into the distance, changing with every season. The landscape is never wild, yet it retains a certain grandeur that is utterly distinct. In summer, the fields are bright with wildflowers, and the gentle hum of bees accompanies the soft rustle of leaves in the breeze. In winter, the hillsides take on a softer, muted beauty, with frost dusting the branches and the occasional mist rising from the streams. It is a place that invites both reflection and activity, as one might choose either a brisk walk across the ridges or a quiet afternoon sketching the view.

At the heart of this countryside lies Pemberley, nestled within its parklands. The approach to the house is, I think, one of the most pleasing aspects of the estate. The road winds gently through the grounds, offering glimpses of the house from afar before presenting it fully at last. The house itself is not ostentatious, though its size and symmetry lend it an air of quiet magnificence. Built of pale stone, Pemberley seems to blend into the very landscape, as though it had grown there rather than been constructed.

The grounds, I must confess, are my favourite part of Pemberley. I have spent countless hours wandering its paths, finding new delights in every season. There is a stream that runs through the park, its waters so clear that one might see the pebbles beneath as though through glass. A small stone bridge crosses it, leading to a shaded grove where the trees form a canopy of green in summer and golden hues in autumn. Farther afield, there are gardens with beds of roses and hedged borders, each one carefully tended yet never overly formal. It is a place where nature feels neither constrained nor neglected, and the air is always alive with birdsong.

THE LIBRARY

Inside the house, one finds a different kind of beauty—one shaped by generations of care. The great library, I think, is one of Pemberley's strongest features. It is a vast room, lined with shelves that rise to the ceiling, filled with books on every subject one could imagine. My brother has taken particular care in expanding the collection, and I often think it is his favourite room in the house. The light that streams through the tall windows makes it a perfect place for reading or studying, and there is always a quiet stillness there, as though the very walls encourage thought and reflection.

Another room dear to me is the music room, where the pianoforte stands. It is a bright and cheerful space, with windows that overlook the gardens. The notes of the instrument seem to fill the room and spill out into the hallways, carrying with them a sense of joy. I have spent many a happy hour there, practicing or playing for my brother and friends. I find great solace in music, and the room seems to lend itself to such pursuits.

A FIREPLACE AND MANTLE AT PEMBERLEY

The dining room, with its long table and appointments, is the setting for many happy gatherings. The portraits on the walls seem to add a sense of continuity, as though the room has always been a place for family and friends to come together. I particularly love the way the light from the chandelier reflects on the polished wood of the table, creating a warm and inviting glow.

The parlour, too, deserves mention, for it is the heart of the house in many ways. It is here that we spend our evenings, reading or conversing by the fire. The furniture is arranged to encourage ease and intimacy, and the walls are adorned with paintings that lend a sense of calm without being overbearing. It is a room where one feels immediately at home, whether resident or guest.

Though Pemberley is a place of considerable size, it is not, I think, imposing. Rather, it carries a feeling of welcome and peace, as though it were meant to be lived in and loved rather than viewed from afar. The people who make up the household contribute greatly to this atmosphere, for they are loyal and kind, and their care for the estate is evident in every detail.

A house as harmonious as Pemberley owes its vitality not only to its architecture and grounds but to the dedicated individuals whose labour and care breathe life into it. Though visitors may admire the polished wood, the tended gardens, and the seamless running of the household, it is the quiet diligence of the staff that makes such refinement possible. Each person plays a part, their efforts weaving together the fabric of daily life at Pemberley.

Mr. Anders, the Estate Steward – At the heart of the estate's operations is Mr. Anders, the steward, a man of quiet authority and unwavering attention to detail. He has served Pemberley for nearly three decades, overseeing everything from the planting of the fields to the management of tenant disputes. Born the son of a tenant farmer on a neighbouring estate, Mr. Anders's aptitude for numbers and a natural sense of fairness caught the attention of the previous steward, who took him under his wing. Now, he is indispensable, balancing the demands of the estate with the needs of the land and its people. His calm demeanour belies the breadth of his responsibilities, and his occasional wry humour is much appreciated by those who work closely with him.

Mrs. Hart, the Housekeeper – Mrs. Hart, the housekeeper, is the undisputed mistress of the household staff, her presence a steadying force within the great house. Though her manner is brisk and her standards exacting, she is deeply respected by those under her charge. She has served at Pemberley for nearly twenty years. Her knowledge of the house is encyclopaedic, and her ability to anticipate the needs of the family and guests is near-magical. Mrs. Hart hails from Derby, where her father worked as a master carpenter, and she speaks fondly of her childhood, though she is fiercely private about her personal life. She is known to carry a small silver locket, a keepsake of her late husband, tucked beneath her collar.

Theresa and the Kitchen Staff – The kitchen, often the warmest and liveliest part of the house, is the domain of Theresa, a formidable woman whose culinary talents are matched only by her sharp wit. Her stews, roasts, and pastries have long been the pride of Pemberley's dining table, and her kitchens hum with activity under her watchful eye. Theresa came to Pemberley from London, where she once worked for a merchant family; her experience in preparing elaborate meals for grand occasions has served her well. Assisting her are a team of kitchen maids, including young Nellie, who is learning to perfect her bread-making under Theresa's stern yet encouraging guidance.

Oliver, the Head Gardener – Outside, Oliver, the head gardener, commands the vast grounds with a passion that borders on devotion. His family has tended Pemberley's gardens for generations. Now, Oliver oversees everything from the cutting of hedges to the planting of seasonal blooms. His knowledge of the land is unparalleled, and his greenhouses are filled with exotic plants he has cultivated with care. Oliver is particularly proud of the rose garden, which he tends with a reverence that suggests he views the flowers as more than mere plants.

Freya, the Parlor Maid – Among the younger staff is Freya, a parlour maid whose quick smile and cheerful nature brighten even the most mundane tasks. She has worked at Pemberley for only two years, having come from a small village where her father was a blacksmith. Freya's lively personality has made her a favourite among the staff, though she is not immune to the occasional scolding from Mrs. Hart for letting her chatter distract her from her duties. She speaks of her dream to one day save enough money to open a small tea shop, a goal she pursues with quiet determination.

Mr. Phineas, the Butler – Presiding over the dining room and ensuring the seamless execution of every formal occasion is Mr. Phineas, the butler. Impeccably dressed and perpetually composed, Mr. Phineas carries himself with an air of dignified authority. His years of experience have made him an invaluable asset, whether arranging the decanting of wine or managing the footmen during a dinner service. Beneath his reserved exterior lies a sharp mind and a dry sense of humour, which he occasionally reveals in private conversations with Mr. Darcy or Mrs. Hart.

The Grooms and Stablehands – The estate's stables are no less integral to its operations, and the grooms and stablehands take great pride in their work. Jack, the head groom, is a wiry man with a quiet affinity for horses. He ensures the family's mounts are always well-cared-for, their coats gleaming and their saddles polished. Young Will, one of the stablehands, has a particular talent for calming nervous horses, a skill that has earned him Jack's praise. Both men are indispensable, ensuring that travel, hunting, and leisurely rides through the grounds are always carried out smoothly.

Each member of the Pemberley staff brings their own history, skills, and dedication to their role, creating a seamless experience for those who live within and visit the estate. They are the ever-present foundation of life at Pemberley, and their quiet contributions ensure that the estate remains not only a place of beauty but one of harmony and purpose. It is often said that a house is only as strong as the people who keep it, and in this, Pemberley is truly fortunate.

In writing this, I find it difficult to convey all that Pemberley means to me, for it is not only a home but a reflection of the values my family holds dear—of care, respect, and harmony with the world around us. I hope that any visitor to Derbyshire might find even a fraction of the peace and inspiration that I feel every day, for it is a place that truly deserves to be seen and cherished.

Lambton: The Warmth of Rural Hospitality — By Mr. Gardiner

LAMPTON TOWN

"To the little town of Lambton, the scene of Mrs. Gardiner's former residence, and where she had lately learned that some acquaintance still remained, they bent their steps, after having seen all the principal wonders of the country; and within five miles of Lambton, Elizabeth found from her aunt, that Pemberley was situated."

Lambton, nestled in the heart of Derbyshire, is a place that seems to embody the charm and simplicity of the English countryside. During my recent visit with my wife and our niece, Miss Elizabeth Bennet, I found myself thoroughly enchanted by the town's gentle rhythm and unassuming beauty. It is a destination that I would most heartily recommend to any traveller seeking respite from the bustle of larger towns, for Lambton offers not only the quiet pleasures of rural life but also the warmth of a community that welcomes visitors as though they were long-lost friends.

Our journey to Lambton, taken during a stretch of fine weather, was marked by the loveliness of the surrounding countryside. The rolling hills of Derbyshire seemed particularly picturesque under the soft light of early summer, their verdant slopes dotted with sheep and bordered by stone walls that spoke of a landscape shaped by generations. As we approached the town, I was struck by its idyllic setting—a cluster of stone cottages and well-kept gardens nestled against the backdrop of gently rising hills.

The town itself is a model of rustic elegance, its streets lined with neat houses of grey stone, many of them adorned with climbing roses or ivy. The marketplace was bustling with activity during our visit, with stalls offering everything from fresh produce to finely crafted goods. I was particularly taken by the friendly demeanour of the townsfolk, who greeted us with smiles and kind words, their accents carrying the unmistakable lilt of Derbyshire. It is a place where life seems to move at a gentler pace, where the pleasures of home and hearth are valued above all else.

Our accommodations in Lambton were at the Lambton Arms, a cozy and well-appointed inn situated near the centre of town. The innkeeper, Mr. Rowley, and his wife, a cheerful and capable woman, made us feel immediately at home. The rooms were clean and comfortable, with feather beds that ensured a restful night's sleep. I found the parlour particularly inviting, with its large fireplace and a selection of books and newspapers that made it an ideal spot for an evening of quiet reading.

The inn's kitchen deserves special mention, for the meals we enjoyed there were among the highlights of our stay. Mrs. Rowley's roast mutton was cooked to perfection, tender and flavourful, and accompanied by a selection of fresh vegetables from the local market. The puddings, served with a rich custard, were equally delightful, and the ale—brewed locally— was of such quality that I could not resist a second pint. It was evident that the Rowleys took great pride in their hospitality, and their attention to detail made our stay all the more pleasant.

During our visit, we also had the great fortune of spending one lovely afternoon at Pemberley, the grand estate of Mr. Darcy. The house, surrounded by sweeping parkland and a lively stream, was as impressive as the man himself—imposing yet full of quiet grace. It was during this visit that my wife and I were first introduced to Mr. Darcy, who proved himself to be a most engaging and thoughtful gentleman. Our initial conversation, marked by his natural reserve and understated warmth, left a favourable impression, and I am pleased to say that our friendship has since grown quickly. Mr. Darcy's deep appreciation for the beauty of his estate and his quiet attentiveness to its every detail reflected a character of strength and depth, one that has endeared him to both my wife and myself.

In addition to the comforts of the Lambton Arms, we had the opportunity to explore the town's other culinary offerings. One afternoon, we dined at the Black Swan, a charming tavern located near the brook. The landlord, Mr. Graves, recommended the game pie, which was richly spiced and paired with a hearty bread that had been baked that very morning. For dessert, we sampled a fruit tart made with berries gathered from the surrounding countryside—a simple dish, but one that captured the essence of the season.

Of course, no visit to Lambton would be complete without taking time to appreciate its natural surroundings. The town is ideally situated for walks and excursions, with paths leading through woods and across fields that offer breathtaking views of the Derbyshire landscape. One particularly memorable outing took us along the banks of the brook, where wildflowers grew in profusion and the sound of the water provided a soothing accompaniment to our conversation. The air was filled with birdsong, and the occasional glimpse of a hare or fox added to the sense of being immersed in nature.

Reflecting on our visit, I am struck by how perfectly Lambton exemplifies the qualities that make the English countryside so beloved. It is a place where beauty and simplicity go hand in hand, where the warmth of human connection is matched by the loveliness of the natural world. The town, with its friendly inhabitants, delightful accommodations, and picturesque setting, is a treasure that I would urge any traveller to discover for themselves. For my part, I look forward to returning to Lambton—and to Pemberley—where I know I shall always find a warm welcome and a sense of peace that is all too rare in our busy world.

A Summer's Journey Through Derbyshire's Countryside — By Elizabeth Bennet Darcy

STAGE COACH PASSENGERS AT BREAKFAST

"The summer was spent in Derbyshire."

My journey to Derbyshire during the summer months, in the company of my dear aunt and uncle, the Gardiners, proved to be an experience of unanticipated delight. Though I have often prided myself on being an observer of human nature, I must confess that the natural world of Derbyshire, in all its summer finery, nearly rivalled my usual preoccupation. With each mile that brought us closer to Lambton, where we were to lodge, I found myself increasingly enchanted by the richness of the countryside, the clarity of the air, and the abundance of beauty that seemed to spring forth from every corner of this remarkable county.

The summer season in Derbyshire is unlike any other I have known, for while Hertfordshire is lovely in its own way, its charms are of a more domestic and predictable nature. Derbyshire, by contrast, possesses a kind of wild elegance—a combination of order and grandeur that feels at once composed and untamed. The hills, clothed in the richest greens and browns, roll with a majesty that inspires thoughts of the eternal, while the valleys are dotted with meadows bursting with wildflowers. The colours seemed almost too vibrant to be real, as if the landscapes had been painted by some master hand, and the scent of the air—sweet with blooming flowers and faintly earthy from the fields—was a tonic for both mind and spirit.

PROPER RIDING DRESS

    Each morning dawned clear and bright, with the sun rising over the hills in a manner so picturesque that it might have been drawn from the pages of Wordsworth's poetry. Indeed, as I watched the soft light spill across the landscape, I found myself recalling his verses: "The world is too much with us; late and soon, Getting and spending, we lay waste our powers." In Derbyshire, however, one feels as though the world is very much with us, and all the better for it.

The days we spent exploring the countryside around Lambton were among the happiest I have known. There is a particular pleasure in walking through fields of tall grass under a sky so blue it seems almost infinite. The warmth of the sun upon one's shoulders, the distant hum of bees, and the occasional burst of birdsong combined to create a symphony that no composer could rival. The paths we followed often led us to unexpected delights: a hidden grove where the air was cool and still, a small waterfall tumbling over mossy rocks, or a view from a hilltop so expansive it took my breath away.

Of course, I must mention our visit to Pemberley, for no account of Derbyshire would be complete without it. The house itself, standing with quiet dignity amidst its parkland, was a marvel of proportion and elegance, and the grounds were nothing short of perfection. The gardens, with their artful blending of the cultivated and the natural, seemed to embody the very spirit of the season, and the stream that ran through the estate added a touch of life and movement to an already enchanting scene.

It was at Pemberley that I had the unexpected pleasure of meeting Mr. Darcy once again, and while our acquaintance had been of a somewhat complicated nature, I was struck during this visit by his kindness and attentiveness. Perhaps the setting of his home, with its beauty and tranquillity, reflected something of his character that I had not before appreciated. Whatever the case, our conversation that day felt easier and more natural than any we had previously shared, and I left Pemberley with a sense of admiration—not only for the estate but for its master as well. I am now blessed to call Pemberley our home.

As I reflect on my time in Derbyshire, I am reminded of the value of stepping away from the familiar and allowing oneself to be surprised. There is a kind of renewal that comes from being surrounded by such beauty, from breathing air that feels purer and walking paths that seem untouched by time. Derbyshire, with its hills and streams, its villages and grand houses, is a place that invites reflection and inspires gratitude. It is a place where the heart feels lighter, where the mind finds clarity, and where one's sense of wonder is restored.

I am grateful to my aunt and uncle for their companionship and their guidance during our travels, for their company made every scene and every moment more delightful. As we returned to Lambton at the end of each day, tired but happy, I could not help but feel that I was storing up memories to carry with me long after the summer had faded.

Stewardship at Pemberley During the Harvest
— By Fitzwilliam Darcy, Esq.

PEMBERLEY IN THE AUTUMN

"The time of harvest brought Mr. Darcy back to his estate."

The harvest season at Pemberley is a time of both labour and reflection, a season that unites all who live and work upon the estate in a common purpose. It is a period of great activity, as the fruits of the year's toil are gathered and stored, and yet it is also a time for gratitude and quiet satisfaction. For a landowner, the harvest is not merely an agricultural event; it is a reminder of the responsibilities inherent in stewardship—responsibilities that extend far beyond the fields and into the lives of those who depend upon the land for their livelihood.

As master of Pemberley, I am acutely aware that the estate is more than a collection of acres, crops, and buildings. It is a community, and at its heart are the people who work the land with diligence and care. During the harvest, I make it my priority to be present among them, for I believe it is not enough to command from a distance; one must see and understand the labour that sustains the estate. To walk the fields as the workers bring in the wheat, to hear the hum of conversation mixed with the rhythmic scything of grain, is to witness the character of these men and women—strong, steady, and resilient in their efforts.

The harvest is no small undertaking, requiring coordination and skill from all involved. The labourers rise early, their work beginning before the sun has fully crested the hills, and they toil until the evening light fades. Each individual has a role to play, from the experienced hands who cut the crops to the younger workers who gather the sheaves. The sight of their cooperation is deeply heartening; it speaks to the strength of a community that understands the value of shared effort.

I have always felt a deep respect for the tenacity and skill of those who work the land. There is a certain dignity in their labour, a sense that they are engaged in something both timeless and essential. They know the rhythms of the earth better than any scholar or gentleman, and their understanding of the seasons and the soil is as profound as it is practical. As I observe them, I am reminded of how dependent I, and indeed all landowners, are upon their expertise and dedication. Without their efforts, the beauty of Pemberley would be but an empty façade, and its prosperity an illusion.

Yet the responsibilities of a landowner extend beyond mere appreciation. It is my duty to ensure that the workers of Pemberley are treated fairly and provided for. Their well-being is inseparable from the health of the estate itself, and I take great care to see that they are paid justly and that their families have the means to live comfortably. During the harvest, it is customary to provide additional provisions—cider for refreshment, hearty meals to sustain their strength—and to celebrate the conclusion of their labours with a feast. Such gestures, while small in comparison to their contributions, are a reflection of the gratitude and respect they so richly deserve.

There is also the broader responsibility of stewardship, which demands that the land be managed with an eye toward its long-term health. To farm recklessly, depleting the soil in pursuit of short-term gain, is to rob future generations of their inheritance. At Pemberley, we employ methods that balance productivity with sustainability, rotating crops and allowing fields to rest when necessary. It is my belief that the land, like the people who work it, must be treated with care and foresight.

The harvest season also offers moments of reflection on the cycles of nature and the continuity of life. To see the fields, once green with growing wheat, turn golden and then be laid bare, is to be reminded of the passage of time and the constancy of change. There is a certain solemnity to this realization, yet it is not without hope. For even as the fields are emptied, they hold the promise of renewal; the seeds sown today will become the harvest of tomorrow.

As I walk the grounds during the harvest, I am often struck by the connection between the estate and the wider world. The grain gathered here will feed not only the workers and their families but also distant markets and households. In this way, Pemberley is part of a larger network, its prosperity intertwined with that of the nation. This interconnectedness is both humbling and inspiring, a reminder that even the most seemingly isolated places have a role to play in the greater scheme of things.

Ultimately, the harvest season is a reminder of the resilience and cooperation of the human spirit. It is a time when differences of rank and station are, for a moment, less important than the shared goal of bringing in the fruits of the earth. For a landowner, it is a season that calls for humility as well as gratitude, for one is reminded of how much depends upon the strength and character of others. At Pemberley, I strive to honour that strength, not only through words but through actions that reflect the values of fairness, respect, and responsibility.

To any traveller who finds themselves in Derbyshire during the harvest, I would urge them to pause and observe the labours of the season. There is a beauty in the sight of a community united in purpose, in the golden fields and the busy hands that bring them to life. And for those who are fortunate enough to call such a place home, the harvest is more than a season—it is a reflection of the bonds that tie us to the land, to each other, and to the future.

The Pleasures of the Fishing Rod:
A Celebration of Angling
— By Mr. Gardiner

"...their progress was slow, for Mr. Gardiner, though seldom able to indulge the taste, was very fond of fishing, and was so much engaged in watching the occasional appearance of some trout in the water, and talking to the man about them, that he advanced but little."

There are few pastimes as rewarding or as contemplative as fishing in the English countryside. To stand by the edge of a clear stream, rod in hand, while the gentle murmur of water flows past, is to experience a harmony between nature and man that is both rare and deeply satisfying. England's rivers, lakes, and streams are uniquely suited to this pursuit, offering not only an abundance of fish but a backdrop of unparalleled beauty. It is a pastime that demands patience and fosters reflection, qualities that align perfectly with the serene landscapes in which it is practiced.

The English countryside, in its quiet elegance, provides the ideal setting for the angler. From the rolling hills of Derbyshire to the tranquil meadows of Hertfordshire, the land seems to invite exploration. The River Wye, with its sparkling waters coursing through limestone dales, is a favourite destination of mine. There, the landscape is as varied as the fish it holds, with wildflowers dotting the banks and the occasional heron standing sentinel in the shallows. Another fine location is the River Test in Hampshire, whose crystal-clear waters are famed for their chalk stream beauty and support a thriving population of trout. It is said that the Test is one of the finest fly-fishing rivers in the world, and I am inclined to agree, having spent many a contented afternoon casting lines amidst its rippling waters.

The native fish of England are among the most esteemed in Europe, their habitats benefiting from the temperate climate and the care with which our waterways are managed. The brown trout, in particular, is a prize of English streams, known for its strength and cunning. To catch one is a challenge that requires both skill and strategy, for these fish are as wily as they are beautiful. The grayling, too, is a delight for the angler, its silvery scales catching the light as it leaps from the water. In the lakes of the Lake District, one may also find pike, a fish of great size and ferocity, whose capture is a triumph of endurance and determination.

What sets English fishing apart is not merely the abundance of its waters but the atmosphere of refinement that surrounds the pursuit. There is a sense of tradition here, a connection to the past that lends the act of fishing a significance beyond the mere catching of fish. Writers and poets have long extolled the virtues of angling, celebrating it as a source of peace and inspiration. One cannot help but feel that to fish in England is to partake in a heritage as old as the rivers themselves.

For those who seek a respite from the demands of life, I can think of no better remedy than a day spent fishing in the English countryside. It is an activity that engages both body and mind, that allows one to appreciate the beauty of nature and the satisfaction of a well-earned catch. Whether in the quiet solitude of a stream or the camaraderie of a fishing party, the experience is one of quiet delight in the splendour of England's waters and landscapes.

Steeped in Tradition:
History and Varieties of English Tea
— By Jane Bennet Bingley

"I confess," said Mr. Collins, "that I should not have been at all surprised by her Ladyship's asking us on Sunday to drink tea and spend the evening at Rosings. I rather expected, from my knowledge of her affability, that it would happen. But who could have foreseen such an attention as this? Who could have imagined that we should receive an invitation to dine there (an invitation moreover including the whole party) so immediately after your arrival!"

Tea, that most cherished of English beverages, holds a place of honour in our homes, our hearts, and our history. Its journey from the far corners of the East to the tea tables of England is a story rich in adventure and refinement, and its role in English society in this year of our Lord in 1813 is nothing short of indispensable. It is my hope that this reflection will illuminate both the origins of tea and the variety of delightful options awaiting the visitor to a proper English tea.

Tea was first introduced to England in the mid-seventeenth century, arriving as an exotic treasure from China and Japan. Its initial reception was one of curiosity and exclusivity, reserved for the elite circles of society. The Portuguese queen consort, Catherine of Braganza, is often credited with popularizing tea in England after her marriage to King Charles II in 1662. Her fondness for the beverage quickly inspired the court to adopt the practice, and tea became a symbol of sophistication and grace. The East India Company imports tea from China, making it increasingly accessible to us British. The varieties of tea are forever increasing, and I will take care to describe may that a visitor to our shores may encounter.

Bohea tea is perhaps the most common black tea in England, coming from the Wuyi Mountains of Fujian Province. It has a rich, smoky flavour and smooth texture, making it a staple for daily consumption. Bohea is often served with milk and sugar, the sweetness complementing its deep, robust profile. It is particularly comforting on a chilly day, evoking the warmth of a hearth and the coziness of a well-laid tea table.

Congou is a finer grade of black tea, and (according to the tea monger in town) takes its name from the Chinese word "gongfu," meaning "skilfully made." Its flavour is smoother and less smoky than Bohea, with a subtle richness that appeals to those who seek refinement in their cup. Congou is an excellent choice for an afternoon gathering, its elegance perfectly suited to the conviviality of polite conversation.

For those who prefer a bolder flavour, Souchong tea offers a deeper, more pronounced smokiness. Made from larger leaves, it is less delicate but no less esteemed. Souchong pairs beautifully with the hearty accompaniments of a traditional English tea, such as seed cakes or buttered bread.

Hyson is a green tea of fine quality. Hyson is named for the English merchant who imported it to great acclaim. Its bright, slightly grassy flavour is both refreshing and invigorating, making it a popular choice during the warmer months. Hyson is best served without milk, allowing its natural sweetness and lightness to shine.

Young Hyson is an even finer version of Hyson, made from the earliest leaves of the tea plant, harvested in spring. It is delicate and refined, with a subtle sweetness that makes it a luxury reserved for special occasions. To serve Young Hyson is to honour one's guest with the finest offering of the tea table.

Gunpowder Tea is so named for the tightly rolled appearance of its leaves, which resemble pellets of gunpowder. This green tea unfurls beautifully when steeped. Gunpowder tea has a crisp and slightly smoky flavour, offering a balance between the delicacy of green tea and the robustness of black tea. It is well-suited to those who appreciate a nuanced and versatile beverage.

The preparation and service of tea are as significant as the tea itself. Water must be brought to a rolling boil and poured directly over the leaves, allowing them to steep for just the right amount of time—too short, and the flavour will be weak; too long, and it may turn bitter. A well-appointed tea service includes a fine teapot, delicate porcelain cups, and all the necessary accompaniments: a sugar bowl, a small pitcher of milk, and, if the host is particularly generous, a plate of lemon slices for those who prefer their tea unadorned by dairy.

The tea table, whether humble or grand, often features a selection of dainties to enhance the experience. Finger sandwiches, seed cakes, buttery biscuits, and scones with clotted cream and jam are traditional accompaniments, each chosen to complement the flavours of the tea. The arrangement of the table, with its tidy elegance and thoughtful presentation, is a reflection of the host's hospitality and care.

Beyond its flavours and forms, tea is a vehicle for connection and civility. The act of offering tea to a guest is an expression of welcome and goodwill, creating a space for conversation, laughter, and the strengthening of bonds. A proper tea visit adheres to the rhythms of politeness: punctual arrival, warm but restrained conversation, and gratitude expressed before taking leave.

For those unacquainted with English customs, tea serves as both an introduction and an invitation. It is a moment to pause amidst the bustle of the day, to savour not only the beverage but the company and the ritual itself. Whether you find yourself enjoying a smoky Bohea, a refreshing Hyson, or a delicate Young Hyson, may your experience of tea offer both comfort and delight, and may it leave you with fond memories of England's cherished custom.

Style and Society:
A Lady's Guide to Country Attire
— By Caroline Bingley

THE TERRACE AT CRACKNILL

"Caroline Bingley's figure was elegant, and she walked in a dress of the newest fashion."

It is common knowledge among polite society—though often lamentably ignored by some—that a lady of refinement and taste must never allow her standards to slip, even when venturing into the rustic charms of the English countryside. Whether one is visiting Derbyshire with its rugged beauty or enduring the more pedestrian scenes of Hertfordshire, one's attire remains a reflection of one's breeding, wealth, and station. To neglect this is to risk the most unpardonable of sins: becoming indistinguishable from the provincial populace. As a woman of society who has observed (and, alas, occasionally endured) the sartorial failings of others, I feel it my duty to guide the less discerning in assembling a wardrobe befitting a proper lady's sojourn in the countryside.

The English countryside, though vastly removed from the sophistication of London or the refinement of Bath, still presents an opportunity for a lady of quality to demonstrate her elegance and superior taste.

WALKING DRESSES

PROMENADE DRESSES

Whether one is promenading along the simple lanes of Hertfordshire or traversing the rugged hills of Derbyshire, one must remember that appearance is paramount, and no detail, however seemingly insignificant, should be overlooked. As I have so often observed, the unfortunate tendency of some ladies to abandon their standards in such rustic settings reflects an appalling lack of awareness. It is my pleasure, therefore, to offer guidance on assembling a wardrobe that ensures one remains a beacon of taste, even when surrounded by the rustic charms of the countryside.

To begin with, a proper wardrobe must include an extensive selection of morning dresses, for nothing is more tragic than a lady forced to repeat an outfit within the same week. Light muslins or cambrics, decorated with delicate embroidery or lace, are ideal for the soft light of a summer morning. Naturally, these dresses must be accompanied by the appropriate undergarments, and I must emphasize the importance of high-quality stays, perfectly fitted. A poorly fitted stay, while tolerated by some, is an unforgivable oversight; it ruins the line of the gown and betrays an utter lack of refinement.

Walking dresses deserve special attention, for the countryside, though picturesque, can be unforgiving to the unprepared. A walking dress must strike the perfect balance between practicality and elegance. A lady's gown should be cut slightly shorter than usual to avoid the indignity of a muddied hem, yet it must never sacrifice beauty. Wool, though durable, should be avoided unless the trimming is of sufficient quality to elevate its appearance. A spencer jacket in a rich hue—forest green or royal blue—is an ideal accompaniment, and one must never forget a fashionable bonnet to shield the complexion from the sun. The bonnet's trimming—whether ribbon, flowers, or feathers—should be chosen with care and, of course, changed daily to match one's outfit.

For social engagements in the evening, a lady's attire must be a triumph of elegance and understated opulence. Silks and satins are de rigueur, and while the country dinner parties and balls may lack the splendour of London assemblies, one must never let down one's standards. Gowns should be adorned with tasteful embellishments— pearls, sequins, or a hint of gold thread. Jewellery must complement, not overpower, the ensemble.

The accessories are equally important and, indeed, reveal the true depth of a lady's refinement. Gloves must be of the finest kid leather or silk, and a lady of taste would never allow her gloves to appear soiled. I must also stress the importance of fans; a well-chosen fan is both a functional tool for cooling oneself and an elegant accessory for communicating wit and charm during social engagements. A fan trimmed with ivory or mother-of-pearl is, in my opinion, indispensable.

Footwear is a detail often neglected by the less discerning, but a lady's shoes are as vital to her appearance as her gown. For walking, sturdy yet fashionable boots are required, preferably in soft leather that flatters the ankle. Slippers for indoor use should be silk, embroidered with fine thread, and changed at the slightest sign of wear. A lady who permits her footwear to fall into disrepair invites judgment on her entire character.

Beyond the necessities of clothing and accessories, a lady must also prepare for her toilette with the utmost care. It astonishes me how many women fail to grasp the importance of preserving their complexion, even in the countryside. A proper lady must bring with her a complete set of cosmetics, though these must be used sparingly to enhance, not mask, her natural beauty. Powder, rouge, and a subtle application of lip pomade are essential, as is a fine scent—rosewater or lavender being my preferences. A silver-handled brush for one's hair is indispensable, as are various combs and pins to ensure that not a single strand is out of place.

Of course, one cannot underestimate the importance of carrying a variety of entirely essential yet often overlooked items. A lady must bring an assortment of ribbons to match every gown, an embroidery kit for moments of idle leisure, and a sufficient supply of scented handkerchiefs, embroidered with her monogram. A portable writing desk is also advisable, for one must be prepared to send notes or invitations at a moment's notice. It is astonishing how many ladies neglect this detail, leaving themselves reliant upon the stationer of whatever rural town they find themselves in—an arrangement that inevitably results in the most dreadful quality of paper.

Lastly, one must not forget the necessity of a well-appointed travelling case. It should be large enough to contain one's essentials yet not so cumbersome as to appear vulgar. A case with compartments for jewellery, perfumes, and minor repairs is ideal. A collapsible parasol should also be included, for while one may hope for good weather, it is better to be prepared for the rain than to suffer the indignity of a sodden bonnet.

Some may find such attention to detail excessive, but let me assure those misguided souls that elegance is in the details. The countryside, while lacking in the sophistication of town, is no excuse for carelessness. A lady's appearance reflects her breeding and character, and to let down one's standards, even in the remotest village, is to risk tarnishing both. Remember, one is always observed, even when one believes oneself alone, and the judgments of others are swift and lasting.

Kent County:
The Garden of England

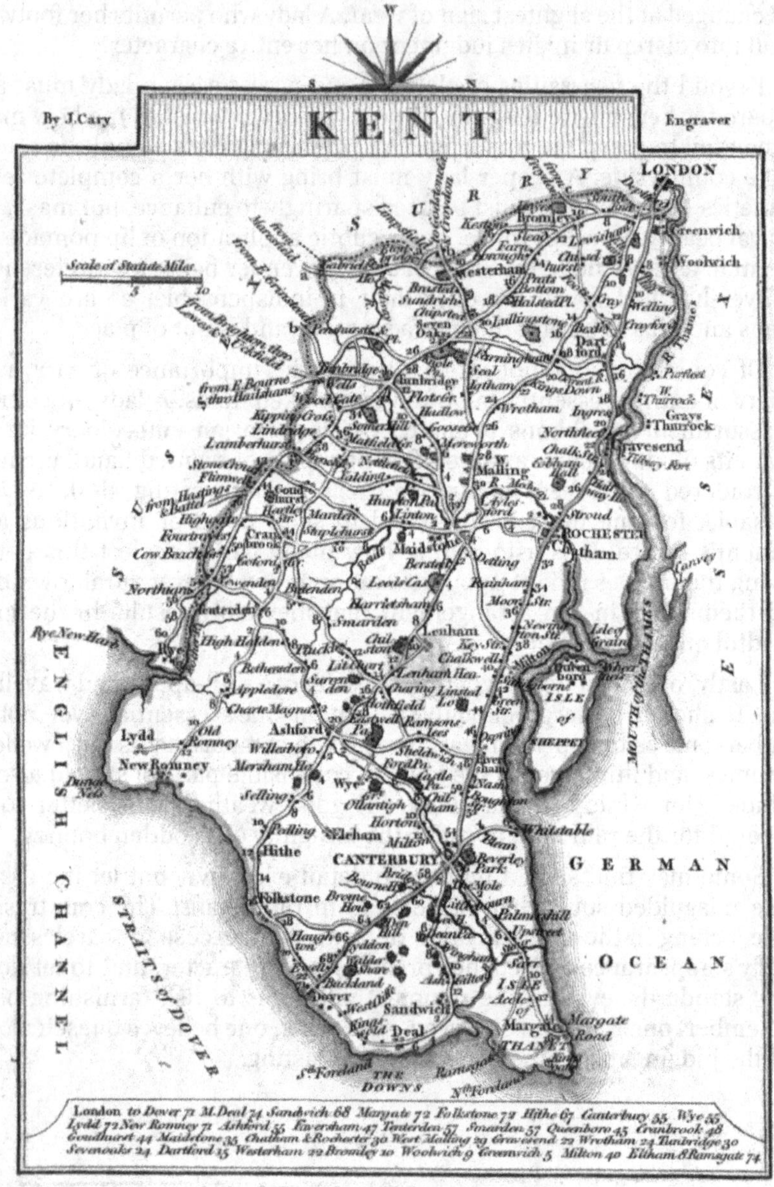

Kent, often called the "Garden of England," lies in the southeastern corner of the country, its fertile landscapes and coastal charm making it a favoured destination for travellers. With a population of approximately 300,000, it is one of England's most picturesque and agriculturally productive counties, renowned for its orchards, hop gardens, and rolling fields.

EXPLORING THE COUNTRYSIDE

Agriculture dominates the Kentish economy, with fruit, particularly cherries and apples, flourishing in its mild climate. Hop cultivation is a growing industry, supplying the brewing trade in London and beyond. The county also has a strong maritime tradition, with shipbuilding and fishing supporting its coastal towns. The naval dockyards at Chatham are of national importance, producing warships that contribute to Britain's maritime supremacy.

Kent is steeped in history, and its landmarks bear witness to its significance through the ages. Canterbury, a city of great antiquity, is the spiritual heart of England and the seat of the Archbishop of Canterbury. Its magnificent cathedral, a masterpiece of Gothic architecture, draws pilgrims and visitors alike. Rochester, another historic city, boasts a Norman castle and a fine cathedral of its own, standing as testaments to the county's medieval heritage.

For those inclined toward the scenic, the white chalk cliffs of Dover are an iconic symbol of England's shores, and Dover Castle, perched high above, offers commanding views of the Channel. The nearby Cinque Ports, including Hythe and Sandwich, once vital to England's defence and trade, remain lively and picturesque.

With its rich history, natural beauty, and bustling industry, Kent offers a delightful balance of heritage and modern enterprise. Travelers will find much to admire in its lush landscapes, historic towns, and coastal splendour, all contributing to its well-deserved reputation as the Garden of England.

Hunsford Parsonage and Its Proximity to Rosings
— By Mr. Collins, Rector of Hunsford

HUNSFORD PARSONAGE

"When they left the high road for the lane to Hunsford, every eye was in search of the Parsonage, and every turning expected to bring it in view…. At length the Parsonage was discernible. The garden sloping to the road, the house standing in it, the green pales and the laurel hedge, every thing declared they were arriving. Mr. Collins and Charlotte appeared at the door, and the carriage stopped at the small gate, which led by a short gravel walk to the house, amidst the nods and smiles of the whole party. In a moment they were all out of the chaise, rejoicing at the sight of each other."

It is with the utmost humility, yet a proper sense of my station and privilege, that I endeavour to describe the many excellencies of Hunsford Parsonage and its situation in the county of Kent. To those unacquainted with the refined and dignified society of this part of England, allow me to assure you that Kent is a county of superior distinction. It is the chosen residence of Lady Catherine de Bourgh, whose advice and benevolent guidance have conferred upon this area, and indeed upon Hunsford Parsonage itself, an air of refinement unmatched in any other part of the country. That I, your humble servant, should be so fortunate as to reside in such a favoured spot is a matter I can only attribute to the blessings of Providence and the unparalleled generosity of her ladyship.

BUCOLIC SPLENDOR

The approach to Hunsford Parsonage is one that inspires a just sense of awe, though modesty forbids me from overextolling its virtues. The roads leading to the village are well-kept, thanks in no small part to Lady Catherine's influence upon the local gentry. They are bordered by hedgerows of remarkable symmetry, interrupted only by the occasional copse of trees that provides a charming rusticity to the view. As one draws nearer to Hunsford, the spire of the parish church comes into view, a sight that, I am sure, fills all who behold it with appropriate reverence. The parsonage itself is situated at a respectable distance from Rosings Park, the grand estate of Lady Catherine, thereby allowing me the great honour of frequent visits to her ladyship while maintaining a respectable independence.

The grounds surrounding Hunsford Parsonage, though not extensive, are, I believe, perfectly suited to a clergyman of my position. A small lawn stretches before the house, bordered by flowerbeds that, while simple, are kept in admirable order—a fact I often attribute to Lady Catherine's wise suggestions on the placement of shrubs and perennials. At the rear of the house lies a small kitchen garden, where the practical meets the picturesque. Here vegetables and herbs are cultivated with care, ensuring both the sustenance of the household and a pleasing addition to the landscape.

The house itself is constructed with such symmetry and good taste that I often think it a model of parochial architecture. Upon entering, one is immediately struck by the proportion of the rooms, which, though small, are arranged with a sense of harmony that is most pleasing. The drawing room, where I receive my guests, is particularly well-situated, with a view of the lawn and the fields beyond. Its dimensions, while not grand, are entirely suitable for a man of my rank and calling.

A CABINET CLEVERLY FITTED WITH SHELVES

Perhaps the most remarkable feature of the house, and one which I am bound to mention with the greatest respect, is the addition of a closet, installed at Lady Catherine's express suggestion. It is a small but invaluable space, perfectly suited for the storage of books, papers, or other articles of utility. Lady Catherine, in her infinite wisdom, observed that such a closet would greatly enhance the functionality of the parsonage, and I have found her prediction to be entirely correct. Every time I open its door, I am reminded of her foresight and benevolence, and I consider it my duty to keep the space in immaculate order as a mark of my gratitude.

The dining room, though not large, is proportioned with a sense of dignity appropriate for entertaining a small party. It has been my honour on several occasions to host Lady Catherine's steward, Mr. Lewis, and other esteemed members of the neighbourhood. The fireplace provides a warmth that is both literal and figurative, creating an atmosphere of welcome and respectability.

In all, Hunsford Parsonage is a dwelling that reflects the best qualities of its surroundings: reservedness, order, and the guiding hand of Lady Catherine de Bourgh. To reside here is an honour I can scarcely deserve but one I endeavour to repay through diligent attention to my clerical duties and the maintenance of my household. I would urge any visitor to Kent to observe the humble charms of Hunsford.

A Humble Tribute to Rosings Park
— By Mr. Collins, Rector of Hunsford

ROSINGS PARK

"Of all the views which Mr. Collins' garden, or which the country, or the kingdom could boast, none were to be compared with the prospect of Rosings, afforded by an opening in the trees that bordered the park nearly opposite the front of his house. It was a handsome modern building, well situated on rising ground."

It is with the deepest humility and the greatest sense of privilege that I undertake to describe Rosings Park, the noble seat of my esteemed benefactress, Lady Catherine de Bourgh. Words are scarcely sufficient to convey the grandeur, refinement, and unmatched elegance of this magnificent estate. Indeed, it is a sight so illustrious, so sublime, that to behold it is to glimpse perfection itself. To be admitted into its august halls, to walk its hallowed grounds, and to enjoy the unparalleled condescension of Lady Catherine's hospitality, is an honour of which I remain ever unworthy but eternally grateful.

The roads leading to Rosings Park are, as one might expect, maintained to the highest standard. The neighbourhood itself is of a most genteel character, its inhabitants deferential to Lady Catherine's superior station and grateful for her guidance. The approach to Rosings is a masterclass in understated magnificence, the long, winding road flanked by ancient oaks and bordered by hedgerows of exquisite symmetry. As the house comes into view, one cannot help but be struck by its grandeur, rising majestically from the landscape, a beacon of taste and authority.

The grounds of Rosings Park are evidence of Lady Catherine's discerning eye and her unparalleled understanding of horticultural elegance. The lawns, which stretch seemingly without end, are as smooth as a fine velvet carpet, and the flowerbeds are arranged with a precision and taste that reflect her ladyship's remarkable sense of order. The shrubbery, so artfully designed, provides both shade and beauty, while the ornamental ponds, complete with swans, lend an air of tranquillity befitting the estate's majesty. It is said that no garden in England compares to Rosings, and having seen it myself, I can only affirm the truth of this statement.

WINDOW CURTAINS AT ROSINGS PARK

Upon entering the house, one is immediately struck by the magnificence of the great room, where Lady Catherine receives her visitors. This room is a marvel of architectural splendour, its ceilings adorned with intricate plasterwork and its walls hung with the finest tapestries. The furniture, though grand, is arranged with an elegance that speaks to Lady Catherine's innate sense of propriety and decorum. It is here that I have had the privilege of receiving her advice on matters both spiritual and practical—advice delivered with such wisdom and benevolence that I count each word as a treasure.

The dining room at Rosings is no less impressive, a space that combines opulence with comfort in a manner only Lady Catherine could achieve. The long table, adorned with gleaming silver and fine porcelain, is a sight to behold, and the meals served there are, as one might imagine, of the highest quality. I must particularly mention the scones, which are, without question, the finest to be found in all of England. Their texture, their flavour, their perfect accompaniment to the tea served in the most delicate china—these are pleasures that linger in the memory and, indeed, in the heart.

A FINE CARRIAGE FOR A FINE LADY

Beyond these principal rooms, Rosings contains a wealth of other spaces, each more impressive than the last. The library is a repository of the most learned and elegant works, a reflection of Lady Catherine's cultivated mind. The music room, adorned with instruments of the finest craftsmanship, is a space where her daughter, Miss de Bourgh, is known to demonstrate her genteel accomplishments, much to the admiration of all who are fortunate enough to witness it.

In all things, Rosings Park reflects the unparalleled refinement and beneficence of Lady Catherine de Bourgh. It is a place that inspires awe, gratitude, and a sense of one's own insignificance in the face of such grandeur. To walk its halls, to tread its grounds, to enjoy even the smallest portion of its hospitality, is to experience the very height of human civilization. I consider it the greatest honour of my life to serve as the clergyman of Hunsford, under Lady Catherine's wise and benevolent patronage, and to live within sight of this most splendid of estates.

For those who have not yet had the privilege of visiting Rosings, I can only say that it is an experience unlike any other—a glimpse into a world of refinement and grace that leaves one forever changed. And for those fortunate enough to be admitted into Lady Catherine's presence, I urge them to approach with the utmost reverence, for they are in the company of a woman whose wisdom, taste, and magnanimity are unparalleled in our time.

Craft and Order:
The Drawing Room Chair of Rosings Park
— by Mr. Collins, Rector of Hunsford

A PARLOR CHAIR AT ROSINGS PARK

"Lady Catherine had even condescended to advise Mr. Collins to marry as soon as he could, provided he chose with discretion; and had once paid him a visit in his humble parsonage; where she had perfectly approved all the alterations he had been making, and had even vouchsafed to suggest some herself, some shelves in the closets upstairs."

I
t is with the greatest reverence and the deepest humility that I undertake the sublime task of describing a chair of such unparalleled perfection as the one that graces the drawing room of Rosings Park. To speak of this chair, designed with the utmost skill and placed under the guidance of my most esteemed patroness, Lady Catherine de Bourgh, is to engage in an act of devotion. For what, indeed, could be more fitting than to celebrate an object that so perfectly embodies the harmony of utility, artistry, and moral purpose?

At first glance, the chair presents itself as a masterpiece of English craftsmanship, a triumph of design and execution that reflects not only the superior taste of Lady Catherine but also the divine order that governs all aspects of creation. The frame, made of the finest mahogany, shines with a rich, warm polish that speaks to the careful labour of the artisan who shaped it. Each curve and angle is demonstration to the principles of geometry, which, as any learned man will tell you, are but a reflection of the Almighty's grand design for the universe. The legs, splayed at an angle of perfect proportion, provide a stability that is both practical and symbolic, reminding us of the importance of steadfastness in both furniture and character.

The backrest, with its elegant arch and delicate scrollwork, is a feature worthy of particular praise. Its curvature, which supports the sitter in an upright position, is not merely a comfort but a moral imperative. For is it not written that man, created in God's image, should conduct himself with dignity and poise? Slouching, I have often observed in my sermons, is a vice that leads to slothfulness of the body and spirit alike. How fitting, then, that this chair should encourage an upright posture, fostering both physical health and moral rectitude in those fortunate enough to sit upon it.

The seat itself, upholstered in a luxurious crimson fabric, offers a softness that is neither excessive nor indulgent. The colour, a deep and noble red, evokes a sense of majesty and refinement, qualities that are, of course, synonymous with Rosings Park and its distinguished mistress. One cannot help but be reminded of the Proverbs' counsel that "strength and dignity are her clothing," a verse that surely applies to both Lady Catherine and this most dignified chair. The padding, firm yet yielding, provides a comfort that allows the sitter to remain composed during even the longest of engagements, whether engaged in polite conversation or in thoughtful contemplation of Lady Catherine's wisdom.

The decorative panel at the centre of the backrest, adorned with an intricate motif, is another feature of profound significance. The design, which appears to represent a stylized floral emblem, is not merely an embellishment but a celebration of the natural world, reminding us of the harmony and beauty that God has bestowed upon creation. It is a detail that elevates the chair from a mere object of utility to a work of art, a reflection of the cultural and moral refinement that Rosings Park so perfectly exemplifies.

The placement of the chair within the drawing room is, I must add, a decision of the utmost genius. Positioned to allow the sitter both a view of the hearth and the opportunity to partake in conversation, it serves as a centrepiece that unites the room's occupants in an atmosphere of comfort and civility. That it resides under Lady Catherine's roof is only fitting, for who else but she could so perfectly embody the principles of taste and propriety that this chair represents?

To sit upon this chair is not merely to rest; it is to partake in an experience that is both physical and spiritual. It is a reminder of the virtues of uprightness, the beauty of craftsmanship, and the blessings of refinement and order. I would urge any visitor to Rosings Park to take a moment to appreciate this remarkable piece of furniture, for in doing so, they will gain not only comfort but also a deeper understanding of the principles that govern civilized life. Such an object, placed in the service of Lady Catherine, is a testament to the heights that humanity can achieve when guided by wisdom, taste, and divine providence.

Easter at Rosings Park
— By Anne de Bourgh

ROSINGS DELICACIES

"At Easter, Mr. Darcy paid his visit to Lady Catherine."

Easter at Rosings Park is always such a special time! Everything feels brighter and prettier, like the whole world is waking up after a long, cold winter. This year's Easter was just lovely, with the gardens starting to bloom and the house filled with all sorts of decorations that Mama planned so perfectly. My cousin Mr. Darcy came to visit, which made it even more wonderful because he is always so kind and polite. Colonel Fitzwilliam came too, and he has such a cheerful way about him that it made everything feel even more festive.

The weather was just right for Easter—sunny but not too warm, with a little cool breeze. When I looked out of my window in the morning, the grass sparkled with dew, and the daffodils in the garden looked so bright and happy. The birds were singing, and I could hear the soft rustling of leaves in the trees. It felt like the perfect kind of day to celebrate something as cheerful as Easter. Even the sky seemed to be in a good mood, all blue with just a few fluffy white clouds.

Inside the house, everything was decorated so beautifully. Mama made sure that every room looked just right, and she is very particular about things like that. There were garlands of ivy and fresh flowers everywhere. I liked the drawing room best, where there were big vases of hyacinths and lilies that smelled so sweet. It made the whole room feel like spring had come indoors. Mama said the flowers were arranged perfectly, and I thought so too. The dining room looked grand as well, with the table set with silver and candles that sparkled like stars.

The food at Easter lunch was absolutely delicious! I don't think I have ever seen a table with so many wonderful things on it. There was lamb that smelled so good, pies with flaky crusts, and vegetables that looked so fresh and green. My favourite part was the simnel cake—it was so sweet and fruity, with a layer of marzipan that was just perfect. The cooks also made little sugar eggs and marzipan animals, shaped like bunnies and birds, which I thought were the prettiest things ever. I saved one of the bunnies because it was too cute to eat right away.

Everyone seemed so happy at lunch. Mr. Darcy didn't say much, but he always listens so carefully when people talk, which I think is very nice of him. Colonel Fitzwilliam told funny stories that made everyone laugh, even Mama, who doesn't laugh very often. It was so nice to have everyone together in the dining room, talking and smiling and enjoying the food.

After lunch, I sat by the window for a little while and looked out at the garden. The sunlight made everything glow, and the flowers and trees looked so lively. It made me think about how much I love living at Rosings Park, where everything is always so lovely and peaceful. Mama works very hard to make sure everything is just right, and I think it shows, especially on days like Easter.

Easter at Rosings Park is my favourite time of year. The flowers, the decorations, the delicious food, and having my cousins visit—it all makes the day feel so special. I hope every Easter can be as lovely as this one, with sunshine and flowers and everyone together.

The Gentleman's Garden:
A Source of Pride and Peace
— By Charlotte Collins

HEARTY ENGLISH PRODUCE

"Mr. Collins invited them to take a stroll in the garden, which was large and well laid out, and to the cultivation of which he attended himself. To work in his garden was one of his most respectable pleasures; and Elizabeth admired the command of countenance with which Charlotte talked of the healthfulness of the exercise, and owned she encouraged it as much as possible."

There is a particular satisfaction, I have come to believe, in seeing a man devoted to the steady and wholesome occupation of tending a garden. Indeed, I would go so far as to opine that every gentleman ought to have his own plot of earth to cultivate. A garden provides not only a diversion from the cares of the world but also a means of engaging with nature in a manner that is at once productive and deeply satisfying. I have observed the truth of this most vividly in my own household, where my dear husband, Mr. Collins, finds unending delight in the progress of his vegetable beds and the orderliness of his garden paths.

It is no exaggeration to say that the garden at Hunsford Parsonage is a labour of love for my husband. From the first days of spring, when the soil is turned and seeds are planted, to the later months when the crops are harvested, Mr. Collins dedicates himself to his garden with a zeal that is both admirable and, dare I say, convenient. He takes great pride in the rows of neatly planted carrots and parsnips, the cabbage heads that swell so handsomely, and the runner beans that climb obediently up their poles. He has, of late, become particularly taken with his potatoes, declaring them the finest in all of Kent—a claim I am sure he would not make lightly.

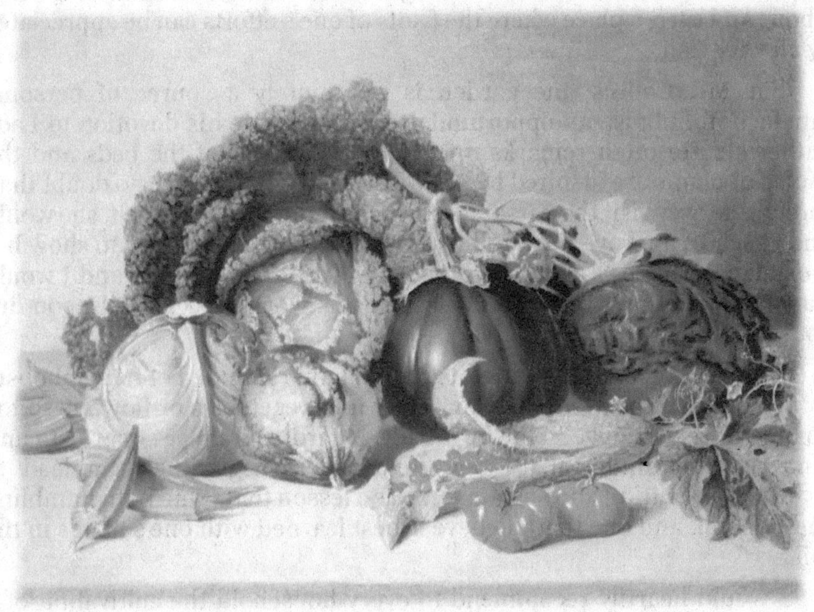

ABUNDANCE FROM THE GARDEN

There is, to my mind, something inherently peaceful about the sight of a man working in his garden. The act of tending the earth, of nurturing plants from seed to fruition, seems to instil a certain calmness and steadiness of character. It is no wonder that poets and philosophers alike have long extolled the virtues of gardening. Mr. Collins himself has quoted to me, on more than one occasion, these lines from Cowper: "Who loves a garden, loves a greenhouse too. Unconscious of a less propitious clime, there blooms exotic beauty." While Hunsford's garden is not adorned with exotic blooms, it is nonetheless a source of beauty and contentment.

I confess that I encourage my husband's horticultural pursuits as often as I am able. The care of a garden requires time and attention, and the rewards of such diligence are many. Not only does Mr. Collins derive great satisfaction from his work, but his endeavours also provide our household with a supply of fresh and wholesome produce. Turnips, onions, leeks, and radishes are among the most frequent fruits of his labour, and their inclusion at our table adds a certain quality to our meals that is both pleasing and economical.

Gardening is, I think, a pursuit well suited to a gentleman. It combines the physical effort of digging and planting with the intellectual satisfaction of planning and nurturing. It requires patience, foresight, and a willingness to accept both success and failure—qualities that are admirable in any man. Moreover, a garden is a visible indication to one's labour and care, a place where the fruits of one's efforts can be appreciated by all who visit.

For Mr. Collins, the garden is not merely a source of personal satisfaction but also an opportunity to demonstrate his devotion to Lady Catherine. He often remarks upon how the layout of the beds and the choice of plants are inspired by her wise suggestions. I have no doubt that, should she ever visit the parsonage to inspect the garden herself, she would find much to approve. Mr. Collins would, of course, be eager to show her the height of his pea plants and the straightness of his rows, and I would stand by with quiet pride, knowing that his work reflects well upon our household.

In reflecting on the value of a garden, I am reminded of its symbolism as well. Just as the seeds we plant grow into vegetables or flowers, so too do the efforts we make in life bear fruit. A garden is a place of growth and renewal, a reminder that even the smallest beginnings can lead to something beautiful and sustaining. It is a lesson that I find both humbling and hopeful, and one that I believe is best learned with one's hands in the soil.

I would heartily recommend to every household the cultivation of a garden. It provides not only nourishment for the body but also peace for the mind and purpose for the spirit. For a gentleman, it is a pursuit of great dignity, and for his family, it is a source of quiet joy. And for myself, I find that the sight of Mr. Collins, hoe in hand and brow furrowed in concentration, is a reminder of the simple and enduring pleasures of life at Hunsford Parsonage.

Fashion at Its Finest:
Admiring the Most Elegant Ladies of My Acquaintance
— By Mrs. Bennet

THE FABRIC SHOPS

"Miss Bingley's feathers nodded in approbation of everything Darcy said."

&

"Mrs. Gardiner, always elegant, adjusted her hat with care before stepping out."

&

"Miss de Bourgh was wrapped in a shawl, though the day was mild, and her mother took care to remind everyone of her delicate constitution."

&

"Lady Catherine was fully attired in velvet and lace, which seemed to demand attention."

There is nothing in this world so delightful as a bit of decoration here, a touch of lace there, or a feather perched just so, to make one feel altogether elegant and noticed. For who does not wish to be admired, I ask you? And truly, there is no better way to accomplish that than by wearing something that demands attention—something that sparkles or flutters or gives everyone reason to look your way. Having had the pleasure of observing the most fashionable ladies of my acquaintance, I simply must tell you about four particular items of apparel that struck me as the very height of refinement and elegance.

Let us begin with Miss Caroline Bingley's decorative feathers, which are always such a sight to behold! Why, when I first saw her with those feathers in her hair at the Netherfield ball, I nearly gasped out loud. Such a clever choice! They were so long and delicate, nodding gracefully with every movement of her head. And how could one not look? They were white, like the purest snow, with little hints of silver that caught the light just so. I could not help but think what a marvellous idea it was to wear feathers, for they seem to elevate a person entirely. Of course, such finery is not so easily come by, and it takes a very fine figure like Miss Bingley's to carry it off properly. Oh, how I wish I had feathers like that when I was younger!

Now, Mrs. Gardiner—oh, what a stylish lady she is! Her hat is the very picture of elegance, so tasteful and so becoming. When she came to visit us at Longbourn, I could not stop admiring it. It was a most charming shade of soft grey, trimmed with a delicate ribbon of deep blue, which set off her complexion to perfection. And the little sprigs of flowers on the side—how enchanting they were! I do believe that hat alone made her look ten years younger. Mr. Gardiner must be very proud to have such a fashionable wife. I only wish I had asked her where she got it, for I should like one just the same for myself, though I daresay my Mr. Bennet would not care a fig for it. Still, a hat like that would surely impress the ladies at the Meryton assembly, and what could be more important than that?

And speaking of impressive, I must not forget to mention dear Anne de Bourgh and her shawl-like headdress. Now, some might say it is a bit too plain for someone of her rank, but I think it is quite elegant in its simplicity. It drapes over her head and shoulders in the most graceful way, as if it were made just for her. The fabric—oh, I am sure it must be the finest silk—has a soft shimmer to it, like moonlight on water. It makes her look so delicate. I thought to myself how clever Lady Catherine must be to have chosen such an accessory for her daughter, for it suits her perfectly.

And now, I must save the best for last—Lady Catherine de Bourgh's velvet and lace attire! Oh, how splendid it was! When we visited Rosings, I could hardly keep my eyes off her. The gown, of the richest black velvet, seemed to command attention, as if to say, "Here is someone of importance." And the lace—oh, such lace I have never seen! It was as fine as cobwebs, with little flowers worked into the pattern, and it framed her face in the most majestic way. Truly, it seemed to demand all attention, and rightly so, for who could be more deserving of admiration than Lady Catherine? I do think there is no one alive who could wear such a gown so well.

It is clear to me that fashion is not merely a matter of clothing but a way to distinguish oneself, to command admiration and respect. Whether it is a feather, a hat, a headdress, or a gown, the right choice can make all the difference. And though I may never have such finery for myself, I take great pleasure in admiring it on others and imagining how grand it must feel to wear it. After all, as I always say, one must make the best of what one has—and if that means dreaming of velvet and lace, then so be it!

Middlesex County:
The Gateway to London

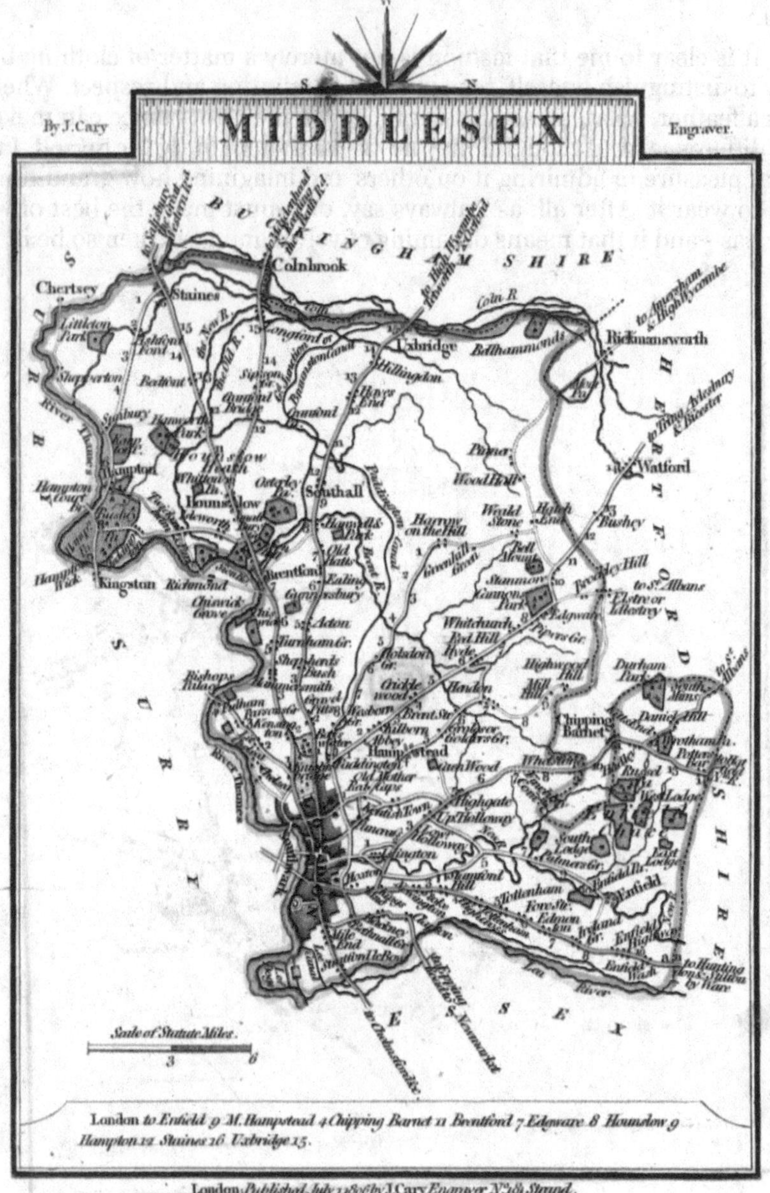

London to Enfield 9 M.Hampstead 4 Chipping Barnet 11 Brentford 7 Edgware 8 Hounslow 9
Hampton 12 Staines 16 Uxbridge 15.

London Published July 1,1806 by J.Cary Engraver N.181 Strand.

Middlesex, a county of strategic importance and bustling activity, serves as the gateway to London, with much of its territory forming the outskirts of the metropolis. Its landscape is a blend of verdant countryside and rapidly growing urban areas, making it a fascinating destination for travellers. The proximity to London ensures that Middlesex plays a key role in supporting the capital. Its economy thrives on a mix of agriculture, trade, and manufacturing. Market gardening is a significant industry, supplying fresh produce to London's bustling markets. The River Thames and the Grand Junction Canal provide essential transportation routes, linking the county's goods to the wider world.

Historically, Middlesex is rich in significance. Hampton Court Palace, once home to Henry VIII, stands as a majestic reminder of the Tudor and Stuart eras. Its grand halls and formal gardens remain a favourite destination for visitors. Nearer to the heart of the county lies the town of Brentford, noted for its role in the Civil War and its busy trading community.

Middlesex boasts the Paddington Arm of the Grand Junction Canal, a marvel of modern engineering that facilitates the movement of goods and people between the countryside and the city. Nearby, the village of Ealing offers a tranquil retreat with its green pastures and rural charm, though it is gradually feeling the influence of London's expansion.

Middlesex is a county of contrasts, where history and progress intertwine.

BULLOCK'S MUSEUM., PICCADILLY

London: The Heart of the Empire

London, the thriving capital of England and the British Empire, is a city unmatched in size, influence, and activity. The metropolis boasts a population of over one million, making it the largest city in the world. A hub of commerce, governance, and culture, London draws people from across the globe to its bustling streets, grand buildings, and thriving industries.

The city's economy is driven by its port, the busiest in the world, where ships laden with goods from the far reaches of the empire dock along the Thames. Trade, banking, and manufacturing flourish, with the East End hosting workshops and factories, while the financial institutions of the City of London manage the wealth of nations. Covent Garden markets teem with fresh produce, and Smithfield is alive with the trade of livestock and meat.

Historically, London is steeped in grandeur. Visitors flock to the Tower of London, steeped in centuries of royal intrigue, and to Westminster Abbey, where monarchs are crowned. St. Paul's Cathedral, a masterpiece by Sir Christopher Wren, dominates the skyline. The Regent's Canal is transforming transport within the city, while the elegant squares of Mayfair offer a glimpse of fashionable life.

Navigating London:
The Path to Distinction and Power
— By Sir William Lucas

METROPOLITAN LONDON

"Sir William Lucas had been formerly in trade in Meryton, where he had made a tolerable fortune, and risen to the honour of knighthood by an address to the king during his mayoralty. The distinction had, perhaps, been felt too strongly.... and, unshackled by business, occupy himself solely in being civil to all the world. For, though elated by his rank, it did not render him supercilious; on the contrary, he was all attention to everybody. By nature inoffensive, friendly, and obliging, his presentation at St. James's had made him courteous."

London, as the beating heart of England, is a city of unmatched significance and splendour. It is a place where rank and influence converge, where opportunities for advancement abound, and where a gentleman of ambition may cultivate the connections necessary to elevate his station. As one who has had the honour of a knighthood conferred upon him—a distinction that has brought both pride and new responsibilities—I feel compelled to offer some guidance to those who seek to navigate the labyrinthine social structures of the capital. It is my belief that such understanding is not only desirable but essential for anyone aspiring to make their mark upon society.

THE LONDON BOARD OF TRADE

The foundation of London's social structure is, of course, rooted in rank and title. It must be understood that a clear hierarchy exists, beginning with the nobility and extending downward through the gentry, the professionals, and, finally, the tradesmen. To know one's place within this hierarchy is to avoid the pitfalls of overreaching or improper familiarity. Titles, land, and lineage are the cornerstones of respectability, and those fortunate enough to possess them hold the keys to the highest circles of society.

For a gentleman, much of one's social capital is determined by one's affiliations. Membership in the right clubs and societies is essential, for these institutions serve as the nexus of power and influence in London. The gentlemen's clubs of St. James's Street, such as White's or Brooks's, are bastions of exclusivity, where the affairs of the nation are discussed and where connections are forged over cards and port. Admission to such clubs is no easy feat, requiring not only sponsorship by existing members but also a reputation that is above reproach. For those fortunate enough to gain entry, the benefits are immense: alliances are formed, reputations are bolstered, and one's presence in the right circles is assured.

NECKCLOTHIANA

Trone d'Amour Tie.*

The *trone d'Amour* is the most austere after the Oriental Tie — It must be extremely well stiffened with starch.† It is formed by one single horizontal dent in the middle. Color, *Yeux de fille en extase.*

Irish Tie.

This one resembles in some degree the Mathematical, with, however, this difference, that the horizontal indenture is placed *below* the point of junction formed by the collateral creases, instead of being above. The color, *Cerulean Blue.*

  * So called from its resemblance to the Seat of Love.

  † Starch is derived from the Teutonick word, "Starc" which means "stiff."

Ball Room Tie.

The Ball Room Tie when well put on, is quite delicious — It unites the qualities of the Mathematical and Irish, having two collateral dents and two horizontal ones, the one above as in the former, the other below as in the latter — It has no knot, but is fastened as the Napoleon. This should never of course be made with colors, but with the purest and most brilliant *blanc d'innocence virginale.*

Equally important are the events and gatherings that constitute the London Season. Balls, dinners, and assemblies provide opportunities to meet individuals of rank and influence, and it is at these occasions that a gentleman's manners and appearance must be above reproach. A well-tailored coat, a carefully chosen waistcoat, and the proper manner of address are as important as one's pedigree. A gentleman who fails to conduct himself with grace and propriety at such events risks not only his own reputation but also that of his family.

In matters of business and politics, London offers unparalleled opportunities for advancement. The courts of law, the financial institutions of the City, and the halls of Parliament are all arenas where a man of ambition may distinguish himself. Yet even in these pursuits, social connections are paramount. To succeed, one must cultivate relationships with those who hold power, for it is through their favour that doors are opened. Patronage, though often criticized by the less fortunate, remains a vital instrument of progress, and a wise gentleman will not hesitate to seek it where it may be found.

One cannot, however, discuss the power structures of London without acknowledging the influence of the fairer sex. Ladies of rank and refinement hold considerable sway in matters of social standing, for it is often through them that alliances are formed and reputations secured. A gentleman must be mindful of his conduct toward ladies, treating them with the utmost respect while recognizing the opportunities they present. A well-chosen marriage, for instance, can elevate a gentleman's position considerably, while a poor match may irreparably damage his prospects.

It is also worth noting that philanthropy and public service are increasingly valued in London society. To be seen as a man of integrity and benevolence is to enhance one's standing, and contributions to charitable causes or participation in civic endeavours are regarded as marks of distinction. While some may scoff at such activities as mere performances, I would argue that they serve a dual purpose: they benefit the less fortunate while demonstrating the gentleman's commitment to the betterment of society.

Finally, I must address the importance of discretion and propriety in all dealings. London, for all its opportunities, is also a city of scrutiny. Gossip and scandal travel swiftly, and even the smallest indiscretion can have far-reaching consequences. A gentleman must therefore guard his reputation jealously, avoiding associations that might tarnish his name and conducting himself with integrity in both public and private matters.

THE MINT

THE ONE POUND BRITISH NOTE

London is a city of boundless potential, but it is also one of exacting standards. To succeed within its social and power structures requires not only ambition and ability but also a keen understanding of the rules that govern its society. By observing these principles—by cultivating the right connections, maintaining impeccable conduct, and seizing opportunities with wisdom and prudence—a gentleman may achieve distinction and secure his place among the ranks of the respectable and influential. For myself, I can only say that the path to success, though often challenging, is one well worth pursuing, for it is in London that the true measure of a man's worth may be found.

The Pleasures of London:
A Resident's Reflections
— By Mr. Gardiner

VIEW OF PICCADILLY
FROM HYDE PARK CORNER TURNPIKE

"It was a journey of only twenty-four miles, and they began it so early as to be in Gracechurch Street by noon. As they drove to Mr. Gardiner's door, Jane was at a drawing-room window watching their arrival.... The day passed most pleasantly away; the morning in bustle and shopping, and the evening at one of the theatres."

London, with all its bustling streets and lively charm, is a city of inexhaustible fascination and opportunity. As a resident of Gracechurch Street, I am fortunate to enjoy not only the convenience of the capital but also the comfort of a home situated amidst its heart. While many may extol the virtues of the countryside—and indeed, there is much to recommend in the simplicity of rural life—London offers a vibrancy and variety that no other place in England can rival. It is a city where one's needs, whether practical or indulgent, are met with ease and efficiency, and where every street seems to hum with the promise of discovery.

Our home on Gracechurch Street is subdued in comparison to the grand houses of the West End, but it is perfectly suited to our needs. Located in the lively borough of Cheapside, it places us within walking distance of many shops, markets, and services. The daily rhythms of London life are both invigorating and endlessly entertaining. From my study window, I often watch as the vendors set up their stalls in the morning, their cries blending with the clip-clop of horses' hooves and the chatter of passersby. There is a constant energy to the street, a sense that something is always happening, which I find most agreeable.

THE GLASSWARE SHOWROOMS

Shopping in London is an experience unlike any other. The variety of goods available is astonishing, from the freshest produce at the markets to the finest silks and muslins at the drapers. One need only stroll a short distance to find everything from books and stationery to hats and shoes, each shopkeeper eager to offer their wares with a mixture of charm and insistence. For those with an eye for fashion, Bond Street and Pall Mall present the latest styles, though one must be prepared to pay dearly for the privilege. Still, there is no denying the thrill of acquiring a well-made coat or a particularly handsome bonnet, knowing that it represents the height of London sophistication.

MIDDLESEX HOSPITAL

The city's dining establishments are equally noteworthy. While our own table at Gracechurch Street is always well-supplied with fine provisions (thanks to my wife's discerning taste and the excellent services of our cook), there is a particular pleasure in dining out. London's taverns and coffee houses offer a variety of fare to suit every palate. At The Cheshire Cheese, one can enjoy a hearty meal of roasted meats and savoury pies, while more refined establishments such as The Crown on Fleet Street serve delicate soups and fine wines. My wife and I have recently discovered a small confectioner near St. Paul's that produces the most exquisite marzipan and sugarplums—an indulgence that has quickly become a favourite.

Of course, life in London comes with its expenses. Goods and services are undeniably more costly here than in the country, but one must consider the convenience and quality that such prices afford. There is a satisfaction in knowing that one's needs can be met at a moment's notice, whether it is the delivery of fresh flowers for an unexpected guest or the tailoring of a coat for an evening's engagement. These are luxuries that are difficult, if not impossible, to obtain in rural areas, and they make London life both comfortable and gratifying.

HOT CROSS BUNNS SELLER, TWO A PENNY

One of the greatest joys of living on Gracechurch Street is the company we are able to enjoy. My nieces, the Bennet girls, have often visited us here, bringing their lively spirits and charming conversation to our household. It is always a pleasure to show them the sights of London, from the grandeur of St. James's Park to the bustling markets of Covent Garden. These visits remind me of how fortunate we are to live in a city that offers so much to its residents and visitors alike.

London is a city of elegance and industry, of refinement and noise, where the latest fashions exist alongside the timeless traditions of English life. For those who are willing to embrace its energy and variety, it offers an experience that is as enriching as it is exhilarating. I count myself fortunate to call it home, and I would encourage any visitor to take full advantage of its many pleasures and conveniences. From the vibrant streets of Cheapside to the stately halls of Westminster, London is a city that never fails to inspire and delight.

From Morning Calls to Royal Galas:
The Proper Wardrobe for a Society Lady in London
— By Louisa Hurst

COVENT GARDEN THEATRE

Mrs. Hurst was a woman of mean understanding and slender accomplishments."

To be a woman of society in London is not merely a matter of birth or wealth—it is an art, a performance, a triumph of taste and refinement over the mundane. The provincial may dream of attending the symphony at Covent Garden, the opera at Drury Lane, or a royal gala at St. James's Palace, but without the proper attire and manners, they are little more than ornamental curiosities in a room of cultivated brilliance. I write this guide not for the women who are already secure in their sophistication but for those who aspire, however vainly, to rise above their humble origins and enter the glittering world of London society.

EVENING DRESSES

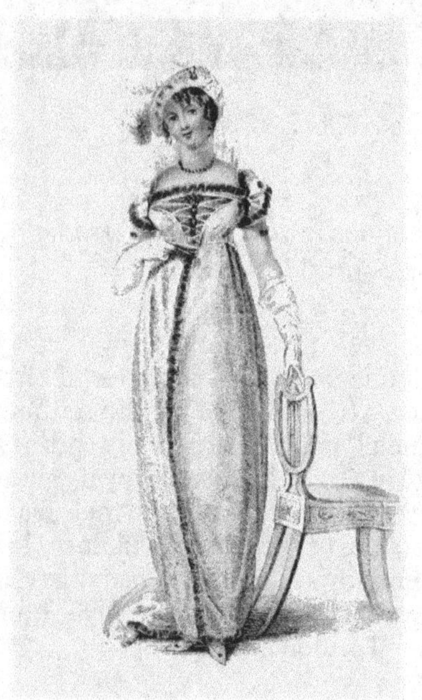

BALL GOWNS

To begin, one must understand that dressing for London is an entirely different matter than dressing for the countryside. While a charming muslin morning gown may suffice for Hertfordshire's muddy lanes, it would be laughably inadequate for the demands of metropolitan life. A proper London wardrobe must be expansive, for each occasion demands its own ensemble, and any woman who dares to appear in the same gown twice within a fortnight will find herself the subject of whispered ridicule.

For morning calls and informal outings, a selection of walking dresses is indispensable. These should be tailored yet elegant, made of fine fabrics such as sprigged muslin or light silk. A floor-length pelisse to cover your outfit in a fashionable shade—perhaps dove grey or pale lavender—is the perfect accompaniment, along with a bonnet trimmed with ribbon and feathers of the highest quality. One must also have gloves of the finest kid leather, for a lady's hands are her calling card, and any sign of neglect in this area is utterly unforgivable.

Afternoon engagements, such as tea with a duchess or a leisurely stroll through Hyde Park, require a slightly more refined ensemble. A visiting gown in rich silk, perhaps adorned with tasteful embroidery or lace, is ideal. Accessories, of course, are paramount. A lady should carry a parasol to shield her complexion from the sun—preferably one with an ivory handle—and a reticule in which to store her handkerchief, a scented vinaigrette box in the event of unexpected swooning or light-headedness, and a small mirror for discreet adjustments. The quality of these items speaks volumes about one's station, and it is better to carry nothing at all than to carry something inferior.

Evening attire is where a lady's true artistry is revealed. For the symphony or opera, one must wear a gown of the finest silk or satin, its cut designed to flatter without vulgarity. Shades of deep blue, burgundy, or emerald are particularly striking under candlelight, though I would caution against anything too ostentatious—after all, one would not wish to appear as though one were attempting to outshine the performers themselves. Jewellery should be carefully selected to complement the gown; diamonds are, of course, always appropriate, though pearls may be worn if one wishes to convey a softer elegance.

For royal galas and other grand occasions, the rules are more exacting still. A ball gown must be nothing short of perfection, with every detail—from the cut of the bodice to the drape of the skirt—calculated to impress. The fabric should shimmer subtly in the light, and the ornamentation—be it beading, embroidery, or lace—should be exquisite but not garish. One's hair must be dressed to the height of fashion, adorned with combs, jewels, or even flowers if the occasion allows.

It goes without saying that a lady must never attend such an event without a gentleman of suitable rank to accompany her. A poorly chosen escort reflects just as poorly on the lady herself.

Beyond clothing, the art of cosmetics must not be neglected. While some may scoff at such enhancements, the discerning woman understands that they are essential to maintaining a flawless appearance. A light dusting of powder to even the complexion, a touch of rouge to enliven the cheeks, and a subtle pomade for the lips are all that is necessary—anything more would verge on the theatrical. A delicate scent, such as rose or bergamot, completes the effect, ensuring that one's presence lingers in the memory long after one has departed.

Social events in London demand more than just the right attire; they require an air of effortless superiority. When attending the symphony at Covent Garden, for instance, one must display an appreciation for the music without seeming overly enthusiastic, for excessive emotion is the mark of a less refined mind. At the opera, one must be seen applauding the prima donna, though not so vigorously as to suggest admiration bordering on envy. And at royal galas, the ability to navigate the room with poise and confidence—while appearing entirely unconcerned by the gazes of others—is an art in itself.

It is, of course, my good fortune to have attended countless such events, and I would humbly venture to say that I have mastered these intricacies. The opportunity to dance at St. James's or to converse with a viscount at a private soirée is, naturally, not one afforded to everyone. Still, for those who aspire to taste the fruits of London society, I offer this advice: strive always for perfection, and remember that appearances are not merely a reflection of one's inner self—they are the foundation upon which one's reputation is built.

Dressing for London is not a matter to be taken lightly. It is a declaration of one's place in the world, to one's refinement and taste. Those who fail to meet its demands are best advised to remain in the countryside, where their deficiencies will be less conspicuous. For those who succeed, however, the rewards are immeasurable—a place among the elite, where beauty and elegance reign supreme.

A Young Lady's Guide to the Art of Conversation
— By Lydia Bennet

"In 1Lydia's imagination, a visit to Brighton comprised every possibility of earthly happiness. She saw with the creative eye of fancy, the streets of that gay bathing place covered with officers. She saw herself the object of attention, to tens and to scores of them at present unknown. She saw all the glories of the camp; its tents stretched forth in beauteous uniformity of lines, crowded with the young and the gay, and dazzling with scarlet; and to complete the view, she saw herself seated beneath a tent, tenderly flirting with at least six officers at once."

To think, I, Lydia Bennet—well, Lydia Wickham now, of course—am here to offer advice to all the young ladies still hoping to find their perfect match. Truly, I am the most fortunate of creatures, for I have secured the most handsome and charming husband in all of England. But it was not mere luck that brought Mr. Wickham and me together; no, it was my mastery of the art of conversation, a skill every young lady must cultivate if she hopes to capture the attention of a suitor.

Now, you must understand that a ball is the perfect hunting ground for eligible gentlemen. The music, the laughter, the swirling gowns—it is all so enchanting! But the true magic happens in the spaces between the dances, when one is seated or strolling and can truly engage a gentleman in conversation. This is where the battle is won or lost, and I dare say I have always been particularly adept at making myself noticed.

The first and most important rule of conversation is to make an impression. Gentlemen do not remember the quiet, demure girls sitting in the corner—they remember the lively ones, the ones with something to say! I shall never forget a ball at Meryton where I found myself partnered with a young officer named Mr. Callahan. He was handsome enough, though of course not as handsome as my dear Mr. Wickham, and he seemed rather shy. Well, I soon cured him of that! I began by remarking on the music, praising the musicians with such enthusiasm that he could not help but smile. "It is impossible not to dance to such a tune," I declared, "though I dare say it would be improved if they played a little faster. Slow dances are for the dull." He laughed—oh, how gentlemen love to laugh—and from that moment, he scarcely left my side the entire evening. Poor Mr. Callahan! He was quite taken with me, though naturally, I had no intention of encouraging him further.

Another key to successful conversation is to show just enough interest in the gentleman without appearing too eager. A well-placed compliment can work wonders, but it must always seem spontaneous. At a ball in Brighton, I found myself speaking to a Mr. Aldridge, a rather serious fellow who clearly thought very highly of himself. "You have such an air of command about you," I said, tilting my head just so, "that I imagine you must be frightfully important in the militia." He looked utterly pleased with himself, and before long, he was telling me all about his great plans for advancement. I listened with wide eyes and exclaimed at all the right moments, though I was mostly thinking about how much more dashing Mr. Wickham looked in his uniform. Still, Mr. Aldridge was so delighted with my attention that he invited me for a second dance, which I graciously accepted—after all, one must never turn down an opportunity to be seen.

Of course, a little flirtation never hurts, so long as it is done with style. Gentlemen like to feel clever, so I often find it effective to tease them just a little. At a garden party in Brighton, I encountered a young lieutenant who was boasting about his skill at cards. "Oh, Lieutenant," I said with a playful smile, "I am sure you must be quite the cardsharp, but I have yet to meet a gentleman who can outwit me at whist." He looked so astonished that I had to laugh, and we spent the next half hour debating the merits of different strategies. By the end of the conversation, he was practically begging me to sit with him at the card table, though, of course, I declined. After all, I had already set my sights on Mr. Wickham, and no one else could compare.

Now that I am a married woman, I can look back on these conversations with pride, knowing that they prepared me for the ultimate victory—winning the heart of my beloved Mr. Wickham. But I must warn my readers that the art of conversation is not without its challenges. One must always be prepared for competition, as there are sure to be other young ladies hoping to catch the same gentleman's eye. The trick is to outshine them without seeming overly bold. A well-timed laugh, a clever remark, or even a small gesture—a touch of the hand, a glance over the shoulder—can make all the difference.

Finally, I must emphasize that confidence is key. A young lady who believes in her own charm will naturally attract the attention of others. At one of the last balls I attended as Miss Lydia Bennet, I wore a particularly lovely gown. I felt so utterly splendid that I could not help but walk into the room with my head held high, and within minutes, I was surrounded by admirers. Mr. Wickham, who had been watching from across the room, later told me that it was at that moment he decided he could not live without me.

The art of conversation is the most valuable weapon in a young lady's arsenal. With a little wit, a touch of charm, and a great deal of confidence, there is no suitor who cannot be won over. And while not every gentleman can be as perfect as my dear Mr. Wickham, I am sure there are plenty of eligible men just waiting to be captivated. So, go forth, young ladies, and make your mark!

The Virtue of Traditional Pianoforte Music — By Mary Bennet

"Mary, after very little entreaty, preparing to oblige the company.... such an opportunity of exhibiting was delightful to her, and she began her song.... Mary, on receiving amongst the thanks of the table, the hint of a hope that she might be prevailed on to favour them again, after the pause of half a minute began another."

In an era where the pursuit of novelty often supersedes the appreciation of time-honoured traditions, it becomes imperative to reflect upon the virtues of classical pianoforte music. The compositions of esteemed masters such as Haydn, Mozart, and early Beethoven embody a purity and balance that resonate with the discerning listener. These works, characterized by their structured elegance and harmonious melodies, offer a sanctuary for the mind and soul—a stark contrast to the tumultuous offerings of contemporary composers.

The fortepiano, the precursor to our modern piano, was the instrument for which these classical compositions were conceived. Its delicate timbre and dynamic range were perfectly suited to the nuanced expressions of the Classical era. Composers like Mozart and Haydn crafted their sonatas and concertos to complement the instrument's capabilities, resulting in music that is both intellectually stimulating and emotionally satisfying.

In recent times, however, there has been a marked shift towards compositions that prioritize technical virtuosity and emotional excess over structural integrity and melodic clarity. The works of certain modern composers, with their relentless cascades of notes and abrupt dynamic shifts, often resemble a cacophony rather than a coherent musical narrative. Such pieces, while perhaps impressive in their technical demands, can overwhelm the listener, leading to an overstimulation of the senses.

It is worth noting that the evolution of the pianoforte into the modern piano, with its expanded range and increased volume, has facilitated this trend towards grandiosity. The iron frame and extended keyboard of contemporary instruments allow for greater string tension and a wider range of dynamics, enabling composers to explore more extreme contrasts in their music.

However, this progression has not been without its detractors. Critics have observed that the emphasis on technical prowess and dramatic expression in modern compositions often comes at the expense of musicality and listener engagement. The intricate passages and rapid tempos can create a sense of agitation, leading to an increase in heart rate and a feeling of restlessness among the audience. Such physiological responses, while perhaps intended to evoke excitement, may instead result in discomfort, detracting from the overall appreciation of the performance.

In contrast, the balanced phrases and clear harmonic progressions of classical pianoforte music promote a sense of tranquillity and contemplation. The measured tempos and graceful melodies encourage a relaxed state of mind, allowing the listener to engage with the music on a deeper, more introspective level. This alignment between musical structure and emotional response is proof of the enduring appeal of traditional compositions.

Furthermore, the moral implications of musical consumption should not be overlooked. Music that incites excessive emotional responses or encourages a loss of self-control can be seen as contrary to the virtues of temperance and modesty. Traditional pianoforte music, with its emphasis on order and propriety, aligns more closely with these moral virtues, offering an edifying experience that uplifts the spirit without compromising one's composure.

AN EVENING CONCERT

While the evolution of musical styles and instruments is an inevitable aspect of cultural development, it is essential to approach such changes with discernment. The virtues of traditional pianoforte music—its structural elegance, emotional balance, and moral alignment—offer timeless benefits that should not be hastily discarded in the pursuit of modernity. By maintaining an appreciation for these classical compositions, we preserve not only a deep musical heritage but also the values that they embody.

On Curating a Gentleman's Library
— By Mr. Bennet

A BOOKSELLER'S SHOP

In his library Mr. Bennet had been always sure of leisure and tranquillity; and though prepared, as he told Elizabeth, to meet with folly and conceit in every other room in the house, he was used to be free from them there.

A gentleman's library serves as both a sanctuary for intellectual pursuit and a reflection of his cultivated tastes. The selection of volumes within such a collection should be approached with discernment, ensuring that each work contributes to the edification and moral fortitude of its reader. Equally important is the exclusion of literature that may undermine these virtues. In assembling a library, a gentleman must exercise judicious selection, favouring works that elevate the mind and spirit while avoiding those that degrade or corrupt. A library should not merely entertain but instruct, inspire, and enrich. It is a reflection of the owner's character and intellect, serving as a beacon of his values and aspirations.

Practical Considerations for Building a Library

Balance of Genres: A proper library includes a variety of genres—history, philosophy, poetry, fiction, and the sciences. This ensures that the gentleman is well-rounded in his knowledge and capable of engaging in discourse on a range of subjects.

Quality over Quantity: While it may be tempting to fill one's shelves with a multitude of volumes, a smaller collection of carefully chosen books will always surpass a larger one of dubious merit.

Preservation of Books: A library should be maintained with care, as the condition of one's books reflects one's respect for knowledge. Keep volumes free of dust, store them upright to avoid warping, and protect them from damp and sunlight.

Accessibility: The arrangement of books should be logical and inviting. History, philosophy, and poetry should be placed in prominent positions, while lesser genres may be tucked into quieter corners of the library.

Essential Works for a Gentleman's Library

"The Works of William Shakespeare"
Shakespeare's plays and sonnets offer profound insights into human nature and the complexities of society.

"Paradise Lost" by John Milton
This epic poem explores themes of obedience, free will, and redemption, challenging the reader's intellect and imagination.

"The Spectator" by Joseph Addison and Richard Steele
A collection of essays promoting virtue and manners, essential for understanding the social mores of our time.

"The History of England" by David Hume
Hume's comprehensive account of our nation's past provides valuable lessons in governance and human behaviour.

"The Decline and Fall of the Roman Empire" by Edward Gibbon
Gibbon's analysis of Rome's fall offers cautionary insights into the vulnerabilities of even the greatest civilizations.

"The Wealth of Nations" by Adam Smith
Smith's treatise on economics lays the foundation for understanding market principles and national prosperity.

"A Vindication of the Rights of Woman" by Mary Wollstonecraft
An argument for women's education and equality, prompting reflection on societal structures and personal prejudices.

"The Poems of Robert Burns"

Burns' lyrical works capture the essence of Scottish culture and the universality of human emotions.

"Travels with a Donkey in the Cévennes" by Robert Louis Stevenson

A travelogue combining adventure with introspection, encouraging a spirit of exploration and self-discovery.

"The Life of Samuel Johnson" by James Boswell

A biography offering a window into the mind of one of England's greatest men of letters.

"The Iliad" and "The Odyssey" by Homer

Epic tales that have shaped Western literature, presenting timeless themes of heroism, honour, and fate.

Works to Exclude from a Gentleman's Library

"Fanny Hill" by John Cleland

A licentious novel that offends decency and offers no redeeming moral or intellectual value.

"The Monk" by Matthew Lewis

A sensationalist tale indulging in grotesque and immoral themes, unfit for refined readership.

"Justine" by Marquis de Sade

A depraved narrative promoting vice and corruption, wholly inappropriate for any virtuous individual.

"The School of Venus" (Anonymous)

An explicit manual of debauchery, serving only to corrupt the mind and spirit.

"The Lustful Turk" (Anonymous)

A vulgar tale exploiting prurient interests, devoid of literary merit or ethical consideration.

"Memoirs of a Woman of Pleasure" by John Cleland

Another of Cleland's scandalous works, perpetuating immoral conduct and lasciviousness.

"The Adventures of King Pausole" by Pierre Louÿs

> A frivolous story that trivializes serious moral issues, unsuitable for a gentleman's contemplation.

"The Satyricon" by Petronius

> An ancient Roman text replete with hedonistic and indecent episodes, offering little of virtuous instruction.

"Gargantua and Pantagruel" by François Rabelais

> While occasionally insightful, its coarse humour and vulgarity render it inappropriate for refined company.

"The Canterbury Tales" by Geoffrey Chaucer

> Though a cornerstone of English literature, certain tales are imbued with bawdy themes unsuitable for all readers.

"The Sorrows of Young Werther" by Johann Wolfgang von Goethe

> A novel that, while influential, has been accused of promoting excessive emotionalism and imprudent behaviour.

"The Confessions" by Jean-Jacques Rousseau

> An autobiographical work revealing personal indiscretions that may be deemed inappropriate for emulation.

A Final Word

The gentleman's library is not merely a repository of knowledge but attestation to his discernment and moral fortitude. By including works that enlighten and challenge the mind while excluding those that corrupt or trivialize, one creates a sanctuary of wisdom and virtue. Let us, therefore, approach the task of curating such a collection with the reverence it deserves, ensuring that our libraries become enduring legacies of our character and intellect.

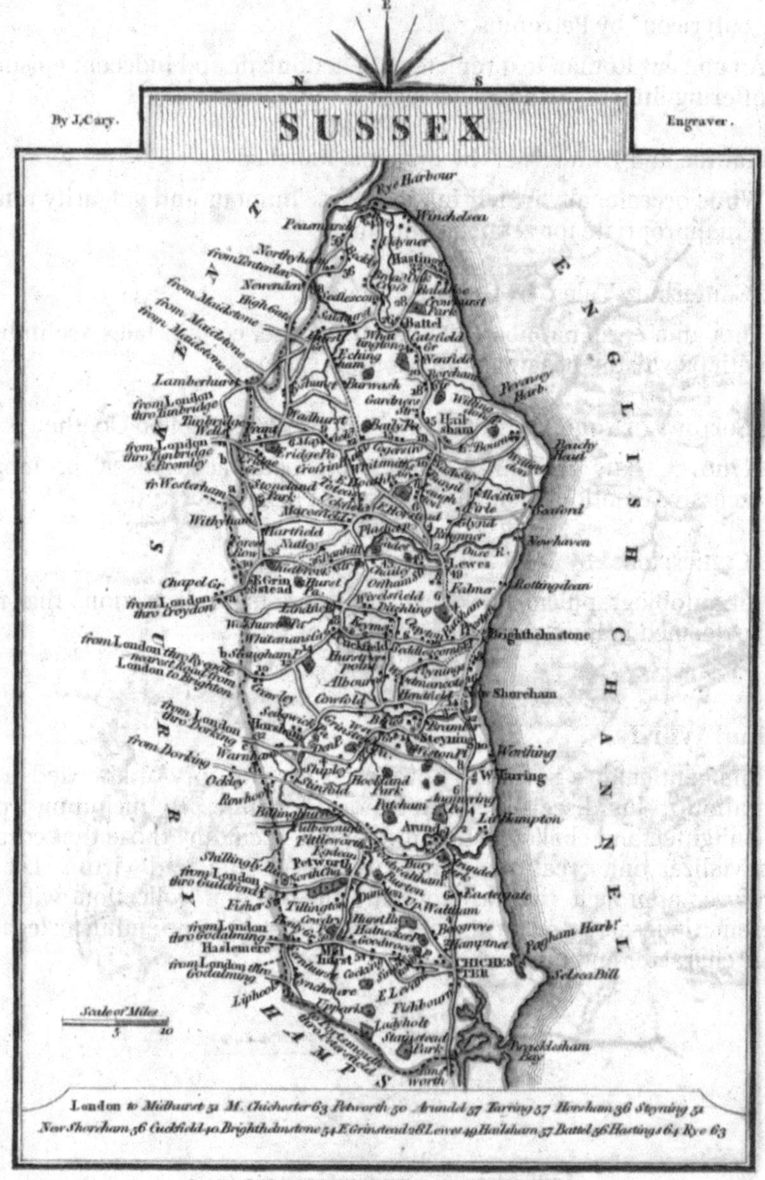

By J.Cary.
Engraver.
SUSSEX
E
N S
Rye Harbour
Winchelsea
Peasmarsh
Iymer
Northyham
Sedle
Hastings
from Tenterden
Newenden
Sedlescomb
Crofd Baldoe
High Gate
Crowhurst
Park
from Maidstone
Salehurst
Battel
from Maidstone
Whatlington
Catsfield
or
Eching
ham
Netfield
Burcham
Lamberhurst
Mayfield
Burwash
from London
thro Tunbridge
Garhurst
Willing
Tunbridge
Wells
Wadhurst
Baly Pa
Hailsham
from London
thro Tunbridge
& Bromley
Frant
E May
Bridge Pa
Crossin
E Oggerth
Whitmans
Bexhill
Pevensey
Harb.
to Westerham
Stoneland
Park
Cotean
Cuckholes
E Hoadly
Peaven
Westham
Beachy
Head
Withyham
Maresfield
E Horsted
Alfriston
Seaford
Hartfield
Plasfield
Rodmer
Great
Row
Nutley
Framfield
Ouse R.
Newhaven
Buckrod
Chailey
Lewes
Chapel Gr.
E Grin
stead
Offham
Falmer
Rottingdean
from London
thro Croydon
Woolsfield
Ditchling
Lindfield
Keymer
Cowfield
Brighthelmstone
Whitemans
Cuckfield
Feildscombe
Staughamp
thurstp
point
Alfning
from London thro Rye gate
nearest Road from
London to Brighton
Albourn
Woomancote
Newtimber
Cramley
Cowfold
Henfield
New Shoreham
Sedgwick
Gris
Bramber
Horsham
Steyning
from London
thro Dorking
Warnham
Weston Pl
Worthing
from Dorking
Shipley
W Tarring
Ockley
Slinfold
Hoatland
Park
Patcham
Angmering
Pa
Rawhook
Billinghu
Littlehampton
Pulborough
Arundel
Fittleworth
Petworth
Bury
Bignoe
Shillingly Pa
Egdean
North Cha
Waltham
Ga
Eastergate
from London
thro Guildford
Barton
Fisher
Tillington
Duncton
Eu
Waltham
from London
thro Godalming
Cowdry
Short Pa
Boxgrove
Hampner
Pagham Harb!
Haslemere
Midhurst
Halnecker
Goodwood
CHICHES
TER
from London thro
Godalming
Cocking
Selsea Bill
Liphook
Penshurst
E Lavant
Fishbourn
Uppark
Ladyholt
Stansstead
Park
Bracklesham
Bay
Elstead
Harting
Worth
Scale of Miles
5   10
ENGLISH   CHANNEL
SUSSEX
SURREY
HAMPS
London to Midhurst 51 M. Chichester 63 Petworth 50 Arundel 57 Tarring 57 Horsham 36 Steyning 51
New Shoreham 56 Cuckfield 40 Brighthelmstone 54 E Grinstead 26 Lewes 49 Hailsham 57 Battel 56 Hastings 64 Rye 63
London Published July 1806 by J.Cary Engraver N° 181 Strand.

Sussex, located on the southern coast of England, offers visitors a pleasing combination of natural beauty, historic landmarks, and industrious communities. The population of the county stands at approximately 200,000, spread across picturesque villages, thriving market towns, and bustling coastal ports. Sussex is a place where the serenity of the countryside meets the invigorating air of the sea, making it a destination for both relaxation and exploration.

The county's economy is anchored in agriculture, with sheep farming on the rolling South Downs producing the finest wool, and fertile fields yielding crops for local and national markets. The coastal towns, including Brighton, Hastings, and Rye, are hubs of fishing and trade, with Brighton gaining particular prominence as a fashionable seaside retreat. The Prince Regent's extravagant Royal Pavilion, under construction in Brighton, is already drawing visitors eager to glimpse its distinctive design and the lively society it attracts.

Sussex is steeped in history, with landmarks that speak to its ancient and medieval past. Arundel Castle, the seat of the Dukes of Norfolk, is a magnificent Norman stronghold overlooking the River Arun, while the ruins of Battle Abbey stand as a solemn reminder of the Battle of Hastings in 1066. The Roman walls of Chichester, a charming cathedral city, echo the county's long history, and its cathedral spire rises gracefully above the town.

Nature lovers will find much to admire in the South Downs, a chalk ridge offering sweeping views of the countryside and sea. The Seven Sisters, dramatic white chalk cliffs along the coastline, are a breathtaking sight and a symbol of England's natural grandeur.

With its rich heritage, scenic beauty, and growing reputation as a fashionable retreat, Sussex is a county that offers something for every traveller.

THE PAVILION AND PROMENADE AT BRIGHTON

Brighton: A Fashionable Seaside Retreat

THE CHAIN PIER AT BRIGHTON

Brighton, a thriving seaside town on the southern coast of England, has grown rapidly in prominence and popularity, transforming from a small fishing village into one of the most fashionable destinations of the Regency era. The population has reached approximately 12,000, evidence of its growing appeal as a retreat for health and leisure.

The town's rise to fame began in the in the 1750s when Dr. Richard Russell extolled the health benefits of seawater bathing and drinking. Brighton became synonymous with restorative sea air and invigorating dips in the waves. The Prince Regent cemented Brighton's reputation when he adopted it as his seaside retreat in the 1780s. His extravagant Royal Pavilion, currently under transformation into a magnificent Indo-Saracenic palace, draws visitors eager to glimpse the splendour of royal taste and indulgence.

Brighton's industries remain tied to the sea. Fishing still sustains many of its residents, though tourism now dominates, with an array of lodging houses, assembly rooms, and bathing machines catering to visitors. The Steine, an open green space near the coast, is a favourite promenade for the fashionable, while the town's growing number of shops and tea rooms provide ample diversions.

Brighton's seaside charm is further enhanced by its location on the English Channel, offering expansive views and bracing winds. The town's pebble beach is bustling with activity, from bathers to entertainers delighting the crowds. For those seeking health, relaxation, or fashionable society, Brighton promises a delightful escape, where the air is fresh, the company lively, and the prospects bright.

Order and Discipline in East Sussex: Brighton's Military Legacy — By Colonel Fitzwilliam

BRIGHTON

" 'They are going to be encamped near Brighton,' Lydia said, 'and I do so want papa to take us all there for the summer! It would be such a delicious scheme, and I dare say would hardly cost anything at all. Mamma would like to go, too, of all things! Only think what a miserable summer else we shall have!' "

Brighton, situated on the southern coast of England in the county of East Sussex, is a town of growing prominence and activity. Known for its bracing sea air and increasingly popular status as a seaside retreat, it also holds strategic importance due to the militia camp stationed there. For those unfamiliar with the customs and operations of English society in 1813, a visit to Brighton offers not only the pleasures of the coast but also a glimpse into the disciplined and orderly life of His Majesty's forces.

The town itself, though not as refined as London, possesses a charm that has attracted visitors seeking health and leisure. The long promenade along the shore provides ample opportunity for walks, the invigorating sea breeze lending strength and vitality to all who partake of it. Brighton's streets, though bustling, are well-kept, and the shops and establishments cater to the varied needs of both residents and visitors. One may find accommodations ranging from simple lodgings to more elegant houses, suitable for families of rank seeking an extended stay.

THE MILITARY COLLEGE

However, the true distinction of Brighton lies in its militia camp, which serves as both a vital military outpost and a symbol of the nation's preparedness. The camp is situated on the outskirts of the town, with its arrangement reflecting the order and efficiency that are hallmarks of the British Army. The tents and barracks are positioned in precise alignment, forming a grid that maximizes both functionality and ease of movement. Such attention to detail ensures that the men are always prepared to act swiftly and effectively should the need arise.

The daily life of the camp is governed by a strict schedule, with activities beginning at dawn and continuing throughout the day. The troops engage in drills and exercises designed to maintain their readiness and discipline, their movements performed with a precision that speaks to the quality of their training. Musket practice, marching formations, and other such activities are conducted under the watchful eyes of their officers, whose role is to ensure that each man fulfils his duty to the utmost of his ability.

THE IRON STEAM SHIP GREAT BRITAIN

It should be noted that the militia stationed in Brighton, though not part of the regular army, plays a crucial role in the defence of the realm. Composed of men drawn from various counties, the militia serves as a reserve force, ready to assist in times of need. Their presence in Brighton is a reminder of the ever-present threats to our shores, as well as the vigilance required to safeguard the nation.

The camp is not without its social aspects, however. The officers, many of whom are gentlemen of education and standing, are often invited to partake in the town's society. Dinners, assemblies, and other gatherings provide opportunities for the blending of military and civilian life, fostering a sense of camaraderie and mutual respect. Such interactions are beneficial, as they remind the troops of the values they are sworn to protect and reinforce the bonds between the army and the people.

For the visitor, Brighton offers a unique perspective on both the pleasures of the seaside and the responsibilities of military service. The town's growing reputation as a place of leisure is well deserved, but its militia camp serves as a sober reminder of the discipline and sacrifice that underpin the security and prosperity of our nation. To observe the camp's operations is to witness the strength and resolve of England, qualities that ensure its continued greatness.

The Art of Adornment:
The Perfect Ribbon and Other Essential Truths for a Lady
— By Catherine (Kitty) Bennet

HATS FOR CARRIAGES AND PUBLIC PROMENADES

"Kitty adjusted the scarf she had borrowed from Lydia, hoping it might gain her some notice."

How important it is for a young lady to understand the power of her attire! A well-chosen hat, a perfectly tied ribbon, or even the colour of one's gown can speak volumes, far more than words ever could. Truly, a lady's appearance is her best introduction, and I cannot imagine how anyone could think otherwise. If a gentleman fails to take notice of your hat or admire the shade of your ribbons, then, I daresay, he is not worth the trouble of pursuing. For how can a man of any sense fail to appreciate such an art as dressing properly?

First and foremost, let us speak of hats, which, I must say, are the crown of a lady's outfit. The shape, size, and embellishments of a hat tell the world precisely who you are. For instance, a large hat adorned with flowers and feathers is sure to command attention in the most delightful way.

But ribbons—oh, ribbons are the most delightful things of all! A lady's choice of ribbon can convey so much about her mood and her intentions. A wide satin ribbon, for example, has an air of elegance and confidence, while a thinner one, perhaps in soft pastel shades, speaks of innocence and charm. When Lydia and I went to Meryton last spring, she bought the loveliest scarlet ribbon for her bonnet, and I must admit it made her look quite daring. I chose a pale lavender one, as I thought it would make me look gentler and more romantic. And do not think for a moment that gentlemen do not notice such things—they most certainly do! A ribbon can draw the eye like nothing else, and I dare say it is often the first thing a suitor observes.

Now, as for bows, they are the most enchanting little details. Whether tied at the waist, on the sleeves, or even at the hem of a gown, a bow can add just the right touch of playfulness. But one must be careful not to overdo it, for too many bows can make one look like a wrapped parcel rather than a well-dressed lady. I am of the opinion that two or three bows are sufficient, placed with great care so as to catch the light when one turns. It is such little details that separate the fashionable from the merely ordinary.

LONDON HEAD DRESSES

And finally, we must consider the colour of a gown, which is perhaps the most important choice of all. Colours speak their own language, and every lady must learn to wield them wisely. Blue is a favourite of mine, as it is both calming and elegant. I wore a light blue muslin to the last assembly, and though I do not wish to boast, I do believe it made my complexion look quite fair. Green, on the other hand, is perfect for garden parties, as it blends so beautifully with the natural surroundings. And red—oh, red is for the bold and daring! Lydia says red makes one look irresistible, though I think it rather too dramatic for my taste. Still, every lady should have at least one red gown, just in case she wishes to make a statement.

A lady's attire is far more than mere fabric and adornment—it is her voice, her charm, her very essence made visible to the world. To dress without thought is to waste an opportunity. I do believe that with the right hat, ribbon, and gown, any lady can secure her future happiness. After all, as I always say, a little care in one's appearance can make all the difference, and who wouldn't want to be the most admired young woman in the room?

The Social Register

The Social Register offers visitors a delightful window into the notable gatherings and lively events of for the years of our Lord 1811 and 1812. For visitors new to the English countryside, particularly as it concerns the public events documented In Miss Austen's work, the Social Register offers a glimpse into the rhythm of rural life, where hospitality and community are always in fashion.

The Meryton Assembly — 15 October 1811

A Spirited Evening in Meryton:
The Assembly Recalled
— By Mrs. Philips

THE MERYTON ASSEMBLY

The Meryton Assembly was a spirited gathering that reminds one of the joys of country life—simple yet charming, lively yet well-conducted. As a lady long acquainted with the society of Hertfordshire, I must say it was particularly gratifying to see such a turnout, not only from our local families but also from some intriguing newcomers who, I daresay, stirred quite a bit of interest among us.

To set the scene for those unfamiliar with our assemblies, allow me to describe the atmosphere. The assembly room was well-lit with a cheerful array of candles that cast a warm glow on the eager faces of the company. The floor, recently polished, gleamed under the feet of our dancers, while the air was filled with the lively strains of the musicians, whose fiddles and flutes enlivened every corner of the room. Decorations were kept to a tasteful minimum—a few sprays of greenery and some colourful ribbons here and there—but the simplicity suited the occasion. After all, in Hertfordshire, we value genial company over unnecessary ostentation.

The event began as all such evenings do, with greetings and introductions as the company assembled. It was during this time that the arrival of Mr. Bingley and his party from Netherfield caused quite a stir. He entered with his two sisters, Miss Bingley and Mrs. Hurst, both of whom were dressed with the kind of London finery that immediately sets one apart in our more modest circles. Accompanying them, of course, was

Mr. Darcy, a friend of Mr. Bingley and a gentleman, whose imposing presence was felt at once. Their appearance sent a ripple through the room, for it is not every day that Meryton plays host to such distinguished guests.

The dancing continued with much merriment, and the company, as always, found ways to amuse itself. My nieces, Kitty and Lydia, were in high spirits, taking every opportunity to engage with the officers of the militia, who added greatly to the evening's liveliness. Indeed, it was impossible not to smile at their youthful enthusiasm. Colonel Forster and the other officers were most obliging partners, and their red coats lent a certain dash of excitement to the proceedings.

The supper was plentiful and well-received. Plates of cold meats, tarts, and jellies were passed around, along with glasses of punch that kept the spirits of the company high. The chatter during the meal was as animated as the dancing As the evening drew to a close, I could not help but feel that the Meryton Assembly had been a success.

The music, dancing, and conviviality left us all with much to talk about in the days that followed, and for that, we must count the assembly a triumph. For those unfamiliar with the customs of Hertfordshire, let me assure you that our assemblies possess a warmth and charm that are uniquely their own, celebrating the spirit of community that binds us together.

The Meryton Militia Parade — 29 October 1811

A Display of Discipline and Duty
— By Colonel Fitzwilliam

OUTSIDE GUARD ST. GEORGES GUARD INSIDE GUARD

The recent militia parade in Meryton provided an excellent opportunity to observe the discipline and readiness of the regiment stationed in the area. Such events are more than mere spectacle; they serve as a public demonstration of the training and preparation essential to maintaining order and protecting the realm. In this regard, the regiment acquitted itself admirably, reflecting the high standards expected of His Majesty's forces.

The parade began precisely at 9:00 with the troops assembling in the town square, where they presented themselves in full uniform. The precision with which the men conducted their drills was commendable, evidencing the rigorous training they have undergone. The cadence of the drums and the clarity of the commands, crisply delivered by the officers, set a tone of discipline and professionalism that was carried throughout the proceedings.

The formation movements demonstrated the regiment's cohesion and attention to detail, as the men executed their manoeuvres with a unity that speaks to their dedication to their duties. This level of coordination is not achieved without considerable effort, and it reflects not only the competence of the enlisted men but also the leadership and diligence of the officers who oversee their training. Such displays are vital, for they reinforce the confidence of the local populace in the militia's ability to maintain order and readiness in times of need.

Colonel Forster, as commanding officer, deserves particular recognition for his steady hand in leading the regiment. His inspection of the troops was thorough. The men responded to his presence with the respect and attentiveness due to a capable leader, and their performance during the inspection reflected his commitment to maintaining a high standard within the ranks.

Following the parade, the regiment conducted a series of coordinated drills, including the presentation of arms and a mock manoeuvre designed to simulate battlefield conditions. These exercises not only showcased the proficiency of the troops but also served as a reminder of the essential role the militia plays in supporting national defence. While some may regard the militia as a secondary force compared to the regular army, their presence and readiness in towns and villages across England are vital to the security of the realm.

It is worth noting the role such parades play in fostering a sense of community and mutual respect between the military and the civilian population. While the focus of the event was, rightly, on the discipline and preparedness of the troops, the presence of local residents provided an opportunity to demonstrate the professionalism of the regiment and to reinforce the bond between those who serve and those they are sworn to protect. These connections are invaluable, for they remind both the military and the civilian population of their shared purpose and common interests.

The Meryton militia has, through this parade, reaffirmed its readiness to fulfil its duties, whether in peace or in the face of future challenges. The discipline displayed on this occasion is a credit to the men and their officers, and it reflects the enduring strength and resilience of England's military tradition. Events such as these are not merely exercises; they are affirmations of the values and dedication that underpin our armed forces, ensuring that they remain steadfast in their role as guardians of the nation.

The Netherfield Ball — 26 November 1811

Elegance Among the Rustic:
Reflections on the Netherfield Ball
— By Caroline Bingley

THE NETHERFIELD BALL

When I look back upon the Netherfield Ball, held some weeks past, I cannot help but take a measure of satisfaction in its execution. Despite the undeniable rusticity of the local society, the evening bore all the marks of refinement and elegance. While the guests themselves may not have been typical of those one might encounter in London, the decor, music, and supper were of a standard befitting the most elevated circles.

The preparations for the ball were nothing short of meticulous. Netherfield's drawing room had been transformed into a space of taste and elegance, its walls adorned with garlands of greenery intertwined with late autumn blooms. The candlelight, softened by crystal chandeliers, cast a warm glow, creating a setting as inviting as it was sophisticated. The effect was such that even the least discerning of our country guests were likely transported into a sphere of greater refinement.

The evening commenced with a flourish, as carriages bearing the local families rolled up the gravel drive. While the arrivals were greeted with all due courtesy, it was, might one say, endearing that our guests, though amiable in their way were unfamiliar with the finer nuances of polite society. Their attire was well-meaning, and refreshing from what might be seen in London or Bath. It was humbling when many of the local company took pains to compliment my own gown, a confection of ivory satin embroidered with silver and my carefully arranged coiffure adorned with diamond pins.

The dancing began shortly after the arrival of all invited guests, with music of excellent quality. A quartet from London had been engaged for the occasion, their skill evident in every note. The local dancers presented a more varied spectacle. My brother Charles, as ever, was the picture of amiability, dancing with nearly every young lady in attendance.

The supper, which I oversaw with the utmost care, was, as anticipated, the crowning achievement of the evening. The long dining table was laden with delicacies that would not have been out of place in the finest London homes. Roasted pheasants, dressed with herbs and accompanied by a selection of sauces, occupied the centre, flanked by tureens of turtle soup and elaborate pastry creations. The pièce de résistance was a towering display of sugared fruits, crafted to resemble a miniature orchard in autumnal splendour. The wines, chosen from my brother's extensive cellar, were of unimpeachable quality. It was gratifying to observe our guests partake with enthusiasm.

The ball, taken as a whole, was a success. The event reflected the grace and grandeur of Netherfield itself. The elegance of the setting and the perfection of the arrangements served as a balm to the occasional rural social norms of our guests. It is a mark of true refinement, after all, to rise above one's surroundings and maintain a standard of excellence regardless of circumstance.

It is gratifying to witness how Netherfield, even if only for one night, brought a touch of sophistication to the rustic environs of Hertfordshire.

The Wedding of Miss Charlotte Lucas and Mr. William Collins — 9 January 1812

A Day of Solemn Rejoicing
– By Mr. Collins, Rector of Hunsford

DANCING THE DEVONSHIRE MINUET

"The marriage took place. The bride and bridegroom set off for Kent from the church door, and everybody had as much to say, or to hear, on the subject as usual."

It is with profound humility and the utmost gratitude to Divine Providence that I, William Collins, Rector of the parish of Hunsford, submit this account of the happiest day of my existence: the day of my union in holy matrimony with the amiable and prudent Miss Charlotte Lucas.

The ceremony took place within the sacred walls of St. Mary's Church, an edifice whose subdued elegance is surpassed only by its spiritual significance. The Reverend Dr. Sanderson, whose exemplary character and theological acumen are well known in the county, officiated with great solemnity. His sermon, a masterly exposition on the sanctity of marriage and the duties incumbent upon husband and wife, left the congregation visibly edified. While some of the younger attendees may have found the discourse lengthy, I can assure them that every moment was a precious gift of enlightenment.

My bride, now Mrs. Collins, entered the church accompanied by her father, Sir William Lucas, whose distinguished bearing—befitting a knight of the realm—was a credit to the occasion. Mrs. Collins wore a gown of unassuming refinement, free from the ostentations that so often mar the simplicity of true virtue. How fortunate I am to have secured a partner who embodies both decorum and sensibility, qualities which I dare say are sadly undervalued in the present age.

A PROPER WEDDING CHAPEL FOR A PROPER RECTOR

The congregation included many notable members of society. Sir William and Lady Lucas were joined by their younger children, who bore themselves with becoming propriety, if not without the occasional signs of youthful exuberance. The Bennet family, with whom I am most favourably acquainted, were unfortunately absent, though I doubt not they shared in the joy of this occasion from afar. Of particular note, Lady Catherine de Bourgh, my esteemed patroness, had graciously conveyed her approval of the match in a letter of unparalleled wisdom and encouragement. Such condescension, I need hardly add, is a testament to her ladyship's superior discernment.

Following the ceremony, the company adjourned to Lucas Lodge for the wedding breakfast, where we were met with a repast that could only be described as both abundant and refined. Sir William, with characteristic generosity, proposed a toast to the happy couple. Though his remarks may have been somewhat embellished by his penchant for eloquence, the sentiment was entirely sincere. His description of marriage as "the highest state of human felicity" was greeted with polite applause, and I could not help but silently concur with his sentiments, considering my own unparalleled good fortune.

The meal was a triumph of domestic hospitality, featuring an array of delicacies that bespoke the Lucas family's good taste and prudent management. The roast pheasant was particularly fine, though I must confess a personal preference for the veal pie, which was seasoned to perfection. The desserts, among which the scones, trifle, and syllabub stood out, were a credit to the cook's skill and industry.

After the repast, the company retired to the drawing-room, where tea was served alongside various entertainments. Sir William delighted all present with his anecdotes of courtly life, drawing comparisons between the ceremonies of St. James's and the homely joys of our gathering. Meanwhile, Lady Lucas presided over the proceedings with her usual grace, ensuring that each guest was attended to with care and consideration.

As the bridegroom, I was, of course, the recipient of many expressions of goodwill and admiration. One guest, a distant cousin of Sir William, remarked that I must be singularly blessed to have secured a wife of such excellent qualities. Though I am not given to vanity, I could not help but inwardly agree with his assessment.

The day concluded with my bride and me departing amidst the well-wishes of our assembled friends and family. We set off for Hunsford Parsonage, where it shall be my life's endeavour to ensure that my dear wife enjoys every comfort and felicity that my position can afford. I am confident that Mrs. Collins will bring great credit to our humble household.

I humbly submit that the union of two individuals, each dedicated to fulfilling their respective duties with diligence and reverence, is a reflection of the Divine Order itself. May our marriage stand as an example to others of the peace and contentment that may be found in a life of piety, propriety, and unshakable fidelity.

The Bennet Family Weddings — 1812

Three Brides, Three Successes:
The Weddings of the Year
— By Mrs. Bennet

*"'My dear, dear Lydia!' Mrs. Bennet cried:
'This is delightful indeed!--She will be
married!--I shall see her again!--She will be
married at sixteen!.... How I long to see her!
and to see dear Wickham too! But the
clothes, the wedding clothes! I will write to
my sister Gardiner about them directly.'"*

*"Mr. Bingley was the happiest creature in
the world, for the day of his marriage had
arrived, and he had Jane for a wife."*

*"Happy for all her maternal feelings was
the day on which Mrs. Bennet got rid of her
two most deserving daughters."*

I t is with the greatest pleasure and no little pride that I take up my pen to recount the most splendid occasions of my life, namely, the marriages of my dear daughters. Indeed, what mother could have been more blessed than I, to see not one, not two, but three of her daughters so happily and advantageously married? Oh, what delight fills my heart, and what satisfaction I feel in knowing that I have done my duty as a mother to secure their futures! Truly, no finer events could be imagined, and I am certain that all who were present will agree with me in every particular.

First, I must tell you of my youngest, my dear Lydia, whose marriage to Mr. Wickham, an officer of such dashing appearance, was the first to occur. Lydia, as everyone knows, has always been full of spirit and vivacity, and it was no surprise to anyone that she should attract the attentions of such a charming gentleman as Mr. Wickham. Their union was a vivid demonstration to the strength of youthful affection, and though it came about rather quickly—oh, what a whirlwind romance it was!—it was clear from the beginning that they were perfectly suited to one another. Mr. Wickham, with his dashing uniform and pleasing manners, has always been held in high regard by those who know him, and his position in the militia speaks to his honourable character.

Though the wedding itself was a private affair, the joy it brought to our family was immeasurable. Upon their return to Meryton, we celebrated their marriage with a gathering at Longbourn, and I could not have been prouder to introduce them as Mr. and Mrs. Wickham. Lydia was radiant, her happiness evident to all, and Mr. Wickham, ever the attentive husband, charmed everyone present with his gracious demeanour. Mr. Wickham, in his handsome regimentals, was the picture of a fine gentleman. His red coat, adorned with brass buttons that shone like the noonday sun, and his bootlaces tied with the most exquisite cord, gave him an air of distinction that made me quite giddy with pride.

It was a day filled with laughter, good company, and the satisfaction of knowing that my youngest daughter had secured such a fine match. I often remind my friends that not every family is so fortunate as to see their daughters married into the military, and I dare say it reflects most favourably on the Bennet name. I was most pleased to note how comfortably Lydia had settled into married life. The ribbons on her bonnet were of the softest satin, and she declared that Wickham was the kindest of husbands, providing her with a new pelisse that was all the rage in Brighton. Oh, how grand it is to say, "My daughter, Mrs. Wickham!"

Now, to speak of my darling Jane, whose wedding to Mr. Bingley was truly the pinnacle of elegance and refinement. Mr. Bingley is one of the most agreeable gentlemen in all of England. The ceremony was held at the church in Meryton, and the whole neighbourhood turned out to witness such a grand occasion. Jane, in her gown of ivory silk, was the very image of an angel. Her veil, oh, such delicate lace, was a gift from Mr. Bingley himself, showing what a thoughtful and generous husband he is.

The wedding breakfast at Netherfield Park was beyond anything I had ever imagined. The table positively groaned under the weight of delicacies: a great ham glazed with honey, and the most delightful assortment of pastries in every flavour, all arranged in perfect symmetry. The napkin rings, which caught my particular attention, were of silver and engraved with tulips and ivy. Such refinement! And Mr. Bingley's manners throughout were impeccable. He made certain that I, as mother of the bride, was seated in the place of honour, and he even complimented the colour of my gown—a most flattering shade of lavender, if I may say so myself.

But the crowning glory of all must be the wedding of my dear Lizzy to Mr. Darcy. Oh, readers, I scarcely know where to begin, for it was a day of such magnificence that I shall remember it all my life. Pemberley, Mr. Darcy's estate, is the grandest house I have ever seen, and I declare it must be twice the size of Netherfield! The ceremony itself was held in the chapel at Pemberley, and I could hardly keep from weeping with joy as I watched my daughter marry a man of such amiable character and consequence.

Lizzy's gown was of the finest white silk, with satin ribbons that fluttered as she walked. And Mr. Darcy—oh, what a sight he was! His tailcoat, with its satin buttons, fit him as if it had been made by angels, and his cravat was tied in the most elegant style. He truly looked every inch the gentleman, and I could not help but feel that Lizzy had made a most brilliant match.

The wedding breakfast at Pemberley was nothing short of a feast for kings. There were roasted pheasants, a whole salmon dressed with herbs, and an array of sweets that seemed never-ending. The butler, a most dignified man, ensured that my glass was always filled with the finest claret, and the servants moved about with such grace and efficiency that one could scarcely believe they were not born to the task.

After the meal, we were given a tour of the house, and I must tell you, dear readers, that the drawing rooms are lined with the most beautiful paintings and tapestries. Mr. Darcy even took the trouble to show me a portrait of Lizzy that had been commissioned for the occasion, and I confess I was quite overcome. Such grandeur, such elegance! And to think that my daughter is now mistress of it all—it is almost more than a mother's heart can bear.

I must say that all three weddings were events of the utmost significance and splendour. Each daughter has done me proud, and I can only hope that my two younger girls will follow their sisters' examples in due time. I can scarcely imagine what joys the future holds, but for now, I content myself with the knowledge that I have three sons-in-law of whom any mother would be proud. And as I always say, a good marriage is the greatest achievement a woman can hope for, and I am fortunate indeed to have played my part in bringing these unions about.

Practical Advice for Travellers

A Practical Guide to Removing Mud and Stains
from a Lady's Garments
— By Mrs. Hill, Housekeeper to the Bennets

"Her petticoat, six inches deep in mud, I am absolutely certain; and the gown which had been let down to hide it, not doing its office."

&

"Mrs. Hill had the advantage of her own personal regard for all the young ladies."

MRS. HILL

A lady's appearance is a reflection of her station and propriety, and nothing mars that impression more swiftly than a stain on her attire. Whether from an afternoon walk through damp fields or an accidental spill at the dining table, stains are inevitable. However, with a little knowledge and prompt action, such blemishes can be removed without damage to the garment. Allow me to share some tried-and-true methods that will ensure every lady maintains her elegance.

General Principles of Stain Removal

Act Quickly: The longer a stain is left untreated, the harder it will be to remove. Address the blemish as soon as it is noticed.

Test the Fabric: Before applying any remedy, test it on a hidden area of the fabric to ensure it does not cause discoloration or damage.

Avoid Rubbing: Always dab or blot stains gently. Vigorous rubbing may spread the stain or damage delicate fabrics.

Removing Mud Stains

Mud is among the most common nuisances, particularly for those who enjoy country walks. Resist the temptation to wipe away wet mud. Instead, let it dry completely. Wet mud can smear and penetrate the fabric further. Once dry, use a soft-bristled brush or clean cloth to gently remove the loose particles. Prepare a solution of lukewarm water with a few drops of mild soap. Dab the stain gently with a clean cloth dipped in the solution, working from the outside toward the centre to avoid spreading the mark. Rinse the area with clean water and blot it dry with a soft towel. Hang the garment in a well-ventilated area to dry completely.

Removing Grass Stains

Grass stains often accompany outdoor excursions and can be stubborn to treat. Mix equal parts white vinegar and water. Dab this solution onto the stain with a clean cloth. If the stain persists, gently rub the area with a bar of pure white soap and rinse thoroughly.

Removing Grease Stains

Grease stains from accidental spills during meals require special attention. Use a clean napkin or paper to absorb as much grease as possible without pressing it further into the fabric. Dust the stain liberally with starch, such as cornstarch or flour, and let it sit for 15—20 minutes. The powder will absorb much of the grease. Brush away the starch, then treat the remaining stain with a solution of soap and warm water.

Removing Wine Stains

Red wine can seem daunting, but swift action ensures success. Dab the area with a clean cloth to absorb as much liquid as possible. Sprinkle salt generously over the stain and allow it to absorb the liquid for an hour. Shake off the salt before washing. For stubborn stains, use a mixture of warm water and vinegar.

By adhering to these practical methods, a lady may confidently preserve her wardrobe's beauty and propriety, ensuring that her garments remain as elegant as her demeanour.

Medicinal Cures for Common Ailments
– By Mr. Jones, Apothecary of Hertfordshire

"The apothecary came; and having examined Miss Jane Bennet, his patient, said, as might be supposed, that she had caught a violent cold, and that they must endeavour to get the better of it; advised her to return to bed, and promised her some draughts. The advice was followed readily, for the feverish symptoms increased, and her head ached acutely. "

MR. JONES, APOTHECARY

As an apothecary serving the good people of Hertfordshire, I have observed that the health of travellers and residents alike can be compromised by the rigors of travel, sudden changes in weather, or simple carelessness in daily habits. It is my duty, therefore, to provide guidance on the causes and remedies for some of the most frequent complaints experienced by visitors to our villages, estates, and towns. Let my observations and advice serve as a companion to those who journey through our fair region.

Colds and Catarrh

Cause: Prolonged exposure to damp or chilly weather, particularly for those unaccustomed to the brisk countryside air. Travellers often fall prey to colds after ill-prepared journeys, as was the case with a young lady I once attended after her wet walk to Netherfield Park.

Symptoms: Congestion, sneezing, coughing, and fatigue.

Remedy: A warm infusion of elderflower and peppermint is most efficacious in relieving symptoms, coupled with rest and a diet of nourishing broth. For stubborn cases, an application of mustard poultices to the chest will draw out the offending humours.

Indigestion and Stomach Complaints

Cause: Overindulgence in rich foods or the consumption of unfamiliar dishes during travel. The feasts at Netherfield and Rosings Park are particularly opulent and may overwhelm the delicate constitution.

Symptoms: Bloating, cramps, and nausea.

Remedy: A draught of peppermint water or an infusion of chamomile will soothe the stomach. For severe cases, a dose of rhubarb powder mixed with honey serves as a gentle purge. Avoid heavy meals and take moderate exercise to aid digestion.

Nervous Complaints and Hysteria

Cause: Emotional strain or excessive excitement, often brought on by social engagements or familial pressures. Such complaints are not uncommon among young ladies preparing for assemblies or balls.

Symptoms: Fainting, palpitations, or heightened agitation.

Remedy: A mixture of valerian root and lemon balm will calm the nerves. Smelling salts, carried discreetly in a reticule, are indispensable for sudden spells of faintness. Gentle walks in the fresh air are highly beneficial for restoring equilibrium.

Headaches

Cause: Overexertion, lack of rest, or prolonged exposure to bright lights and noisy gatherings.

Symptoms: Dull or throbbing pain in the temples or forehead.

Remedy: Apply a compress soaked in vinegar and rosewater to the forehead. An infusion of feverfew is particularly effective for persistent headaches. Quiet repose in a shaded room is essential for recovery.

Aches and Pains from Travel

Cause: Long hours spent in carriages over uneven roads, such as those leading to Lambton or Brighton.

Symptoms: Stiffness, soreness, and general discomfort.

Remedy: Rubbing the affected areas with oil of camphor or a tincture of arnica will provide relief. A warm bath infused with rosemary or lavender is also recommended to ease tension in the muscles.

General Preventative Advice

Hydration: Drink plenty of water or barley water, particularly after travel or exertion.

Diet: A balanced diet of simple, wholesome foods will fortify the constitution. Avoid excessive consumption of rich pastries and heavy meats.

Rest: Adequate rest is vital to maintaining health, especially after social engagements or long journeys.

Cleanliness: Regular bathing and the use of lavender water or rosewater on the skin will promote both hygiene and well-being.

I trust this guide will prove invaluable to visitors exploring the various locales mentioned in our esteemed county and beyond. Whether traversing the lively streets of Meryton or the serene grounds of Pemberley, let prudence and preparation guard your health. Should you require further assistance, I remain at your service in Meryton, ready to dispense remedies and counsel with the utmost care.

An Essay on the Proper Conduct and Contentment for Women of Modest Birth
– By Lady Catherine de Bourgh

A MOTHER AND HER CHILDREN

" 'My daughter and my nephew are formed for each other,' said Lady Catherine de Bourgh. 'They are descended on the maternal side, from the same noble line; and, on the father's, from respectable, honourable, and ancient, though untitled families. Their fortune on both sides is splendid. They are destined for each other by the voice of every member of their respective houses; and what is to divide them? The upstart pretensions of a young woman without family, connections, or fortune. Is this to be endured! But it must not, shall not be. If you were sensible of your own good, you would not wish to quit the sphere, in which you have been brought up.'"

It is with a sense of duty and benevolence that I, Lady Catherine de Bourgh, address this essay to young women of lesser birthright, who might benefit from guidance on their station in life and the virtues of accepting their natural place within the ordered structure of society. The wisdom of centuries has established that harmony is preserved when each individual remains within the sphere to which Providence has assigned them. For women of the middle classes, this truth should be embraced with gratitude and a steadfast sense of duty.

It is not given to all to enjoy the privileges of rank and wealth. Such blessings, bestowed sparingly, are not the fruits of mere chance but the design of Providence itself. To aspire to rise beyond one's station is to defy the natural order, and such defiance is often met with ruin. Women of modest birth must, therefore, temper their ambitions and find fulfilment in the roles appointed to them—namely, as dutiful wives, caring mothers, and respectable members of their community.

The desire for more—whether it be influence, luxury, or recognition— leads not to happiness but to dissatisfaction and impropriety. It is unbecoming of a woman to neglect her obligations in favour of idle dreams, and it is a disservice to her family and society to seek that which was never hers to claim.

For women of the middle classes, the home is a sanctuary wherein their virtues may shine. A well-managed household, a cheerful hearth, and the proper upbringing of children are the hallmarks of a life well-lived. These accomplishments are as noble in their own way as the great estates of the aristocracy, for they contribute to the stability and prosperity of the nation.

Young ladies should take pride in their domestic skills, their modest accomplishments, and their ability to bring comfort to those around them. These are the qualities that commend a woman to her peers and, more importantly, to her family. The pursuit of higher status through inappropriate alliances or pretensions of grandeur diminishes these virtues and brings no true satisfaction.

History offers countless examples of the perils faced by those who seek to rise above their station. Women who endeavour to attach themselves to men of superior rank often find themselves the subject of ridicule or, worse, disgrace. Such unions, when they occur, are rarely harmonious, for the disparity in education, manners, and expectations creates a gulf that no affection can bridge.

Furthermore, such attempts to rise often result in the neglect of one's own family and class, leading to estrangement and a loss of the respect that should be every woman's most cherished possession. The consequences of such folly extend beyond the individual, sowing discord and discontent throughout society.

Let it not be said that I wish ill upon those of modest birth. On the contrary, I hold a firm belief that true happiness lies in the contentment of fulfilling one's appointed role. To marry within one's own class, to raise a family with diligence and care, and to grow old with the esteem of one's neighbours—these are the blessings that ensure peace of mind and a lasting legacy.

A young woman who accepts her place in life with humility and grace will find that her days are filled with purpose and her heart with joy. The envy and ambition that trouble so many are banished by the simple act of embracing one's natural station.

To those who would argue that birth and rank are but accidents of circumstance, let me remind them that society is upheld by order and tradition. To seek to overturn these foundations is to invite chaos and diminish the very fabric of our existence. Women of lesser birth should therefore view their station not as a limitation but as a calling, one that carries its own dignity and rewards.

Remember, young ladies, that your worth is measured not by the heights to which you climb but by the fidelity with which you fulfil your duties. To be content with mediocrity, as some might term it, is no shame; it is, in truth, the virtue of recognizing that a modest life, well-lived, is sufficient to earn the respect of your community and the favour of Providence.

I trust that this advice will serve as a beacon of guidance to those who might otherwise stray from the path of propriety. Accept your station, perform your duties with diligence, and you shall find that the respect of others and the peace of your conscience are rewards far greater than the fleeting pleasures of ambition.

On the Education of Women:
A Father's Reflections
— By Mr. Bennet

THE HALL AT HERALDS COLLEGE

"'No governess! How was that possible?' asked Lady Catherine de Bourgh. 'Five daughters brought up at home without a governess!--I never heard of such a thing. Your mother must have been quite a slave to your education.'

Elizabeth could hardly help smiling, as she assured her that had not been the case.

'Then, who taught you? who attended to you? Without a governess you must have been neglected.'

'Compared with some families, I believe we were; but such of us as wished to learn, never wanted the means,' Elizabeth said. 'We were always encouraged to read, and had all the masters that were necessary. Those who chose to be idle, certainly might.'"

It is seldom acknowledged that society's greatest disservice is its treatment of women—not as equal partners in intellect and wit, but as lesser beings whose sole purpose is to charm, obey, and serve. As a father of five daughters, I have observed with both amusement and despair the absurd expectations placed upon women. They are taught from their earliest years to suppress their intelligence, to silence their opinions, and to view themselves as ornaments to men's lives, rather than full participants in their own. It is a notion so limiting, so counter to reason, that one wonders how England, a nation of such pride and accomplishment, has not crumbled under the weight of this folly.

Allow me, then, to indulge in a radical notion: that women should be educated—not simply in accomplishments that please the eye or ear, but in the same breadth of knowledge and reason as men. While such an idea may seem fantastical to the conservative mind, I hold that society would be vastly improved if women were allowed to cultivate their intellects and pursue their potential as rational beings.

At present, the education of women is directed almost exclusively toward superficial accomplishments. They are taught to play the pianoforte, to sketch landscapes, to speak French or Italian, and to embroider flowers upon cushions. These are pleasant diversions, to be sure, but they are hardly sufficient preparation for the trials of life. A woman may sing prettily or paint a charming scene, but of what use are these talents when her husband falls into financial ruin, or her children require guidance and discipline? How can she be an equal partner in a marriage when she is taught only to submit, never to reason?

Moreover, the enforced ignorance of women is an insult to their natural abilities. I have seen my own daughters demonstrate sharp wit, penetrating insight, and a capacity for learning that rivals any man's. Yet society insists that such qualities are unbecoming in a woman. They are told to laugh softly, to speak rarely, and to yield always. It is a waste of human potential so profound that one cannot help but despair at the loss.

If women were properly educated, the benefits to society would be manifold. First and foremost, they would become better wives and mothers, capable of contributing to their families not merely as caregivers but as equals in thought and judgment. A woman who can reason, plan, and understand the world is far better equipped to manage a household, guide her children, and support her husband in times of trouble. An educated woman would enrich society as a whole. Imagine a world where women could conduct experiments or engage in politics—not as novelties or exceptions, but as equals to men. Their perspectives, shaped by experiences unique to their gender, would bring new insights and innovations to every field of human endeavour. England's progress, both intellectual and moral, would surely accelerate if half its population were no longer confined to ignorance.

The education of women would elevate the character of men. A man who is accustomed to conversing with intelligent women will learn to respect their minds and value their opinions. He will no longer seek a wife who is merely beautiful or obedient but one who is his equal in thought and spirit. Such marriages, based on mutual respect and shared understanding, would be far happier and more stable than those founded on inequality.

I am not so naive as to believe that such a transformation in society would be easily achieved. The entrenched prejudices against women's education are as old as the hills, and those who benefit from the current system—chiefly men—will not relinquish their privileges without a fight. To educate women is to challenge the very foundations of our social order, and many would rather see England crumble than entertain such radical ideas.Indeed, there are those who argue that educating women would make them dissatisfied with their roles, that it would encourage them to neglect their families, or that it would make them unfit for marriage. These objections are, in my view, baseless. A woman who is educated is no less capable of loving her children or managing her household. On the contrary, she is better equipped to do so with wisdom and efficiency. As for marriage, any man who fears an intelligent wife is a man unworthy of one.

Though I am sceptical that England will embrace the education of women in my lifetime, I cannot help but imagine a future where it is the norm. In this future, women will write books that inspire nations, solve problems that confound men, and lead lives of purpose and fulfilment. They will no longer be judged solely by their beauty or accomplishments but by the strength of their minds and the content of their characters.

It is a vision as hopeful as it is unlikely, for I know too well the stubbornness of tradition and the fear of change. Yet I take solace in the small victories—the spirited arguments of my daughter Elizabeth, the clever remarks of her sisters, and the quiet defiance of every woman who refuses to be silenced. These are the seeds of change, and though they may take generations to bear fruit, they are planted nonetheless.

To deny women an education is to deny humanity half its potential. It is a folly so glaring, a waste so profound, that one must question the wisdom of those who defend it. If England is to remain a great nation, it must embrace the talents and intellects of all its people, regardless of gender. Let us not fear the collapse of society but rather the stagnation that comes from refusing to grow. For in the education of women lies the promise of a brighter, more equitable future—and that is a vision worth striving for.

An Essay on the Qualities of an Accomplished Woman — By Fitzwilliam Darcy, 1804

<u>Originally published in 1804</u>

Prologue from Fitzwilliam Darcy, Esq., December 1, 1813

It is not without some consternation, even piercing embarrassment, that the essay presented herewith was penned by me during my younger years while a student at Eton. Regrettably at the time I shared my admittedly misguided and naïve perspectives regarding the stature and role of women in a civilized England. As this was previously published in the Eton Journal during my university years, this book's publisher and certain individuals whom I hold in the utmost respect have encouraged me to share this work once again, in the hopes that it will be illustrative and informative to influence today's man to eschew such Byzantine, patriarchal beliefs as I have since abandoned. With respect, I implore you to provide me the courtesy of reading the more recent essay I wrote that follows this piece of drivel on the pages that follow after.

I remain your humble servant,

Fitzwilliam Darcy, Esq.

&

"'A woman must have a thorough knowledge of music, singing, drawing, dancing, and the modern languages, to deserve the word; and besides all this, she must possess a certain something in her air and manner of walking, the tone of her voice, her address and expressions, or the word will be but half deserved,' cried the faithful Caroline Bingley.

'All this she must possess,' added Darcy, 'and to all this she must yet add something more substantial, in the improvement of her mind by extensive reading.'

'I am no longer surprised at your knowing only six accomplished women,' said Elizabeth. 'I rather wonder now at your knowing any.'"

A GAME OF CHESS

I t should be evident to any man of reason that the selection of a wife is
not merely a matter of inclination but of the gravest consequence to his
station, happiness, and the preservation of his lineage. A gentleman of
my position and sensibility cannot be content with mediocrity in this vital
matter; the woman who claims his heart and hand must exhibit a degree
of refinement and capability that elevates her above the common herd. In
this essay, I shall delineate the qualities that constitute the ideal woman—
qualities which, though rare, are indispensable in one who would claim the
distinction of being an accomplished lady.

To be considered accomplished, a woman must possess more than
mere beauty or charm, though these are, of course, pleasing attributes. The
essence of accomplishment lies in a combination of intellectual
cultivation, social grace, and practical skill. She must demonstrate an
elegance of mind that speaks to her education and understanding, for no
amount of physical allure can compensate for a deficiency of intellect. A
lady without wit is no more than a finely dressed ornament, pleasing to the
eye but devoid of substance.

An accomplished woman must excel in the finer arts. Her proficiency
in music, her skill in drawing, her command of modern languages—these
are not merely frivolities but marks of her refinement and the diligence of

her upbringing. A woman who has devoted herself to such pursuits reveals a discipline and a respect for culture that are essential to her role as a companion and mistress of a household.

Beyond intellectual and artistic accomplishments, an ideal woman must exhibit the highest standards of decorum and comportment. She should conduct herself with a dignity befitting her station, speaking and acting with a grace that inspires admiration without ostentation. Her manner must strike a delicate balance—neither overly familiar nor excessively reserved, neither insipidly timid nor unseemly bold.

In her interactions, she must demonstrate a keen understanding of social nuance, capable of charming and engaging all whom she meets. A woman who lacks the ability to navigate the complexities of society, who cannot shine in company or sustain intelligent conversation, cannot hope to fulfil the role of a gentleman's wife. She must be as adept in the drawing-room as she is in the quiet study, proving herself a credit to her husband in all arenas of life.

Above all, an ideal woman must possess an unblemished moral character. Her principles must be as firm as they are virtuous, her conduct as irreproachable as her reputation. She must inspire respect and trust, not only in her husband but in all who know her. A lady who lacks integrity, whose behaviour is frivolous or insincere, brings dishonour not only upon herself but upon her family and, by extension, her husband.

Though I have spoken at length of the qualities of mind and character, let it not be supposed that physical beauty is without importance. While it may not form the foundation of a woman's worth, it is an adornment that enhances her other virtues. A pleasing countenance, a graceful figure, and an elegance of dress—all these contribute to a lady's appeal and render her more captivating to her husband and to society. Yet, beauty alone, unaccompanied by intellect or virtue, is a fleeting and insubstantial quality, insufficient to sustain lasting affection or respect.

It is often said that women of true accomplishment are exceedingly rare, and I must concede the truth of this assertion. Many young ladies are content with mediocrity, indulging in idle diversions rather than striving to perfect themselves. They rely upon their beauty or their connections to secure advantageous marriages, without considering the duties and expectations such a union entails.

A man of discernment cannot settle for such inadequacy. His wife must not only complement him but elevate him, enhancing his life with her wit, her elegance, and her unerring judgment. To unite oneself with a woman of lesser qualities is to risk not only personal dissatisfaction but public embarrassment—a prospect intolerable to any gentleman of pride and principle.

It has been my privilege to encounter a variety of women in the course of my life, and though I have seen many who possess some of the qualities

I have enumerated, few embody them all. This is, perhaps, as it should be, for perfection is a lofty ideal, and the pursuit of it demands both patience and discernment. Yet, I cannot help but believe that a man who values his own worth must demand excellence in his partner.

To those who would accuse me of undue pride or unattainable standards, I can only say that my expectations are born not of vanity but of conviction. A gentleman who understands the gravity of marriage, who respects both himself and his future family, cannot afford to compromise. The woman who meets these standards, rare though she may be, is worthy of both admiration and devotion, and it is for such a woman that I am willing to wait.

It is with this belief that I stand resolute, for while others may yield to the temptations of mediocrity or the whims of passion, I shall remain steadfast in my pursuit of a wife who exemplifies the highest ideals of accomplishment and character. To settle for anything less would be unworthy of a man of my station, and, indeed, of a man of any discernment at all.

On the True Qualities of an Ideal Wife
— By Fitzwilliam Darcy, Esq., 1813

"Occupied in observing Mr. Bingley's attentions to her sister, Elizabeth was far from suspecting that she was herself becoming an object of some interest in the eyes of his friend. Mr. Darcy had at first scarcely allowed her to be pretty; he had looked at her without admiration at the ball; and when they next met, he looked at her only to criticise. But no sooner had he made it clear to himself and his friends that she had hardly a good feature in her face, than he began to find it was rendered uncommonly intelligent by the beautiful expression of her dark eyes. To this discovery succeeded some others equally mortifying.

Though he had detected with a critical eye more than one failure of perfect symmetry in her form, he was forced to acknowledge her figure to be light and pleasing; and in spite of his asserting that her manners were not those of the fashionable world, he was caught by their easy playfulness. Of this she was perfectly unaware; to her he was only the man who made himself agreeable no where, and who had not thought her handsome enough to dance with.

He began to wish to know more of her, and as a step towards conversing with her himself, attended to her conversation with others. His doing so drew her notice."

It is often said that time and reflection are the greatest instructors, and I, having experienced both, find myself compelled to revise many of the notions I once held regarding the nature of the ideal wife. While youth and inexperience may prompt a man to value accomplishments, beauty, and social graces above all, greater wisdom teaches that these are but ornaments to a far deeper substance. The qualities that make a wife truly ideal cannot be measured by the superficial standards of society, but by the depth of her character, the strength of her mind, and the sincerity of her heart.

An ideal wife must, above all, be her husband's equal—not merely in station or accomplishments, but in intellect and spirit. She must possess a mind capable of understanding and challenging his own, for what companionship can endure if built upon condescension or dullness? A wife whose wit and intelligence shine brightly brings not only delight but improvement to her husband's life, for her perspectives broaden his own and her arguments refine his judgment. Such a woman is a partner in every sense of the word, offering not blind agreement but thoughtful discourse, which is the foundation of true harmony.

Equally important is a wife's integrity and strength of character. A woman who knows her own mind and adheres steadfastly to her principles is far more admirable than one who bends too easily to the will of others. Her courage in the face of adversity and her willingness to speak truth, even when it is unwelcome, are marks of a character both noble and unyielding. Such a woman inspires not only love but respect, for her moral compass remains unwavering even in the most trying circumstances.

SHARING A WALTZ

This strength of character often reveals itself in kindness and generosity, for a woman of true worth is not only steadfast in her principles but also compassionate to those around her. She brings light and warmth to all who know her, her goodness extending beyond her family to friends, neighbours, and even strangers. It is this blend of strength and gentleness that renders her presence a balm to the soul, a source of comfort and inspiration.

Though many might overlook it, I believe that a shared sense of humour is among the most vital qualities in an ideal wife. A woman who can laugh at life's absurdities, and who can bring her husband to laugh at himself, possesses a rare and precious gift. In her company, the burdens of the world feel lighter, and the joys more profound. Her wit is never cruel, but always playful, and her laughter is a melody that brightens the darkest days. It is through laughter that a wife and husband forge a bond of intimacy that no trial can break, for humour is a sign of understanding, of seeing the world through each other's eyes.

An ideal wife is not perfect, for perfection is an illusion that no human being can attain. Rather, she is someone who strives always to grow, to learn, and to better herself—and who encourages her husband to do the same. She has the humility to acknowledge her faults and the courage to overcome them, just as she offers grace and forgiveness when her husband falters. In her, one finds the embodiment of hope and renewal, a partner who inspires not only affection but transformation.

Finally, the ideal wife is one whose love is steadfast and enduring. It is not a love built on fleeting passions or empty flattery, but on a deep and abiding connection that weathers every storm. Her love is patient and forgiving, but also honest and challenging, for she loves her husband not as he is, but as he could be. She sees his flaws and mistakes but believes in his potential, offering both support and accountability. In her love, one finds not only comfort but the courage to become a better man.

It is a curious thing to look back upon one's former beliefs and see how far they fall short of the truth. Once, I believed the ideal wife to be a woman of accomplishments and beauty, a figure to be admired but not necessarily understood. Now, I see that the true measure of a wife lies not in her accomplishments but in her heart, her mind, and her spirit.

The ideal wife is a woman whose presence enriches every moment, whose wisdom and kindness uplift all who know her, and whose love transforms her husband into the best version of himself. She is not merely a companion but a partner, not merely a figure of admiration but a source of inspiration. To know such a woman is a privilege; to love her is a blessing beyond measure.

Though I have no intention of singling out any individual, I can say with certainty that such women do exist, rare though they may be. Their worth cannot be measured by society's standards, for they possess a greatness of soul that transcends such trivialities. To those fortunate enough to have such a wife, I would say only this: treasure her, for she is a gift beyond all reckoning.

The Unwritten Rules:
A Woman's Guide to Etiquette
— By Jane Bennet Bingley

While English women are celebrated for their elegance, wit, and devotion to domestic harmony, they might one day be known for something even more remarkable: their influence beyond the drawing room and the tea table. I would like to imagine a world where women are not merely the ornaments of society but its architects— contributors not only to the gaiety of a ball but to the betterment of their communities and, dare I say, their nation. Such notions might seem lofty or even laughable to some, but allow me to suggest that this is not such an impossible dream.

Let us first consider education. At present, the pursuit of knowledge is not wholly denied to women, but it is often confined to those arts deemed most suitable for pleasing a husband or managing a household. Accomplishments such as playing the pianoforte, paintingqui tables, or crafting a particularly fine piece of embroidery are all very well in their way, but they are hardly the highest aspirations of an inquiring mind. Might not a young lady benefit from the study of history, philosophy, or even the natural sciences? Imagine the conversations that could arise if we were allowed to discuss the works of Locke or Newton alongside the merits of lace or muslin. A well-educated woman is, I dare say, a more engaging companion, and what man of sense would prefer a dull wife merely because she is silent? The notion is absurd.

If education were more expansive, we might see women contributing not only to the domestic sphere but also to the broader intellectual life of the nation. There are matters of great importance—charity, commerce, and even politics—where a woman's perspective might prove invaluable. One cannot forget that women, as mothers, sisters, and wives, are natural observers of human character. Their insight into the motivations and follies of others is unmatched, and such wisdom could easily be applied beyond the family circle. My father, for all his cynicism, often remarks on the absurdities of human behaviour; surely he would admit that a woman's perspective might offer solutions to such follies if only she were permitted to speak freely.

And speak freely we must. At present, a woman's opinion, however intelligent, is often dismissed as irrelevant or improper. I have been accused more than once of speaking my mind too plainly, and while I do not regret it, I recognize that not all women are so fortunate as to have their impertinence tolerated. But imagine a society where this were not the case, where a young lady might debate the merits of a new law or propose improvements to her village without fear of being thought unwomanly. Surely, such a world would be richer for it.

Let us take, for example, the subject of charity. Women are already the primary managers of charitable efforts, whether organizing soup kitchens or assisting the sick. These tasks are important and honourable, but why should they be limited to the private sphere? Might not a woman's administrative skills be applied to broader endeavours? Perhaps one day, we shall see women advising Parliament on matters of social reform, using their firsthand knowledge of the poor and disadvantaged to shape policies that truly serve the nation. A fanciful idea, perhaps, but not beyond the realm of possibility.

Consider the example set by great women of history—queens, poets, and philosophers—who have shaped their times through their intellect and determination. If young girls were taught from an early age that their minds are as valuable as their appearances, might they not grow into women capable of great things? And if society were to recognize and reward such women, others would surely follow their example. It seems to me that this is not a question of what women are capable of but what they are allowed to pursue.

The subject of marriage is, of course, one that cannot be ignored. While a single man in possession of a good fortune is assumed to be in want of a wife, it is equally true that the happiness of such unions depends on mutual respect and understanding. A well-educated woman, confident in her opinions and secure in her abilities, is far better equipped to be a true partner to her husband. A man who values his wife's intellect as much as her beauty is far more likely to find happiness in his marriage. Perhaps one day, society will recognize that an intelligent wife is not a liability but an asset.

It is also worth noting that these changes need not diminish the qualities that are already celebrated in women. A lady may be educated and opinionated without losing her charm or grace. Indeed, is not the most captivating woman one who combines beauty with intelligence? The notion that intellect and elegance are mutually exclusive is as laughable as it is false.

I propose a humble vision for the future: a world where young women are not merely asked how well they play or sing but how wisely they think and act. Where mothers teach their daughters not only the art of needlework but also the value of curiosity and courage. Where men and women stand as equals—not in physical strength, of course, for nature has its limits—but in intellect and moral worth. Such a vision may seem fanciful to some, but to those of us who dare to dream, it is a future worth striving for.

Until that day comes, I shall continue to speak my mind, to read my books, and to delight in the company of those who value wit and wisdom above all else. And I encourage any young lady who reads this to do the same. For if we do not imagine a brighter future, who will?

Beyond the Drawing Room:
A Vision for England's Daughters
— By Elizabeth Bennet Darcy

A young woman of respectable station must navigate the intricate world of social gatherings with grace, charm, and, above all, propriety. Yet, behind the rustle of silk gowns and the murmur of polite conversation, there lies a question worth pondering: to what extent must a woman conform to the expectations laid before her, and where might she find room to assert her individuality?

Allow me to guide you through the labyrinth of etiquette and expectation, not merely with the aim of ensuring your success in society, but also with the hope of encouraging a quiet yet steadfast fidelity to your true self.

At the heart of every social gathering lies an unspoken contract: to participate is to adhere to its unwritten rules. Whether attending a grand ball, an intimate dinner, or a simple tea, a woman is expected to comport herself with dignity and decorum, her every action reflecting credit upon her family and her upbringing. To speak too much is to risk seeming immodest; to speak too little is to invite the judgment of being insipid. To dance too freely is to appear frivolous; to refuse to dance is to risk being labelled proud or aloof. Every gesture, every word, is measured against the yardstick of propriety, and the weight of these expectations can be heavy indeed.

And yet, I must confess, there is a quiet defiance in me that bristles against the notion that a woman's worth is determined solely by how well she performs this societal dance. The truth is that many of these expectations, though they masquerade as rules of civility, often serve to constrain rather than liberate. They demand that a woman suppress her wit, her intellect, her very essence, all for the sake of pleasing those who might never truly know her.

Let us consider, for instance, the expectation that a young woman must always present herself as agreeable. While civility and kindness are virtues to be admired, there is a fine line between being agreeable and being compliant. How often are women encouraged to stifle their opinions, to smile and nod in silent acquiescence, even when their hearts burn with dissent? Politeness, I argue, need not come at the expense of authenticity. A woman may disagree without being disagreeable, and it is entirely possible to voice one's thoughts with both conviction and tact.

The art of conversation, too, is fraught with contradictions. Women are expected to charm, to entertain, to keep the conversation light and pleasing, but not to delve too deeply or speak too earnestly. Yet, I cannot imagine a world in which a woman's mind, with all its complexity and depth, is not allowed to shine. There is joy to be found in an exchange of ideas, in a debate that is spirited but respectful, and in the discovery of a kindred spirit who appreciates one's intelligence as much as one's manners.

Even in matters as seemingly innocuous as dress, the weight of expectation is keenly felt. A gown must be elegant but not ostentatious, flattering but not immodest. While I understand the value of presenting oneself well, I often wonder why so much emphasis is placed on a woman's appearance, as if the fabric of her gown could ever be more important than the substance of her character. Dress, like conversation, should be an expression of one's individuality, a reflection of one's personality and taste. To dress purely to please others is to don a costume, and I would much rather wear the garment of my choosing than one dictated by the whims of society.

Of course, there are those who will argue that these expectations serve a purpose, that they bring order to the chaos of human interaction and create a framework within which society can thrive. To some extent, I agree. Manners and customs, when practiced with sincerity, are the oil that smooths the wheels of social interaction. But when these customs become a cage, binding women to roles that deny them their individuality, they do more harm than good.

I urge my fellow sisters to tread the path of social gatherings with both care and courage. Embrace the customs that bring joy and connection, but do not allow them to stifle your spirit. Dance when you wish to dance, but let it be for the sheer pleasure of the movement, not because you feel it is expected of you. Speak your mind, but do so with kindness and grace. Wear the gown that makes you feel most like yourself, whether or not it conforms to the latest fashion.

Above all, remember that within the most structured of gatherings lies the opportunity for true connection and meaningful exchange. It is not the rigid observance of every rule that creates lasting impressions, but the warmth, sincerity, and individuality you bring to the room. Let your light shine in a way that is uniquely yours, for the truest elegance lies in authenticity.

Let us find strength in the knowledge that we are not merely performers in society's grand play but authors of our own characters. Each choice we make—whether to speak, to laugh, to listen, or to remain silent—shapes the story we tell to the world. May yours be a tale of courage, grace, and a heart unbound by fear.

Yours most faithfully,

Elizabeth Bennet Darcy